mISKIN gIRL

aLYSON yOUNG

First published in Great Britain 2016 by Lynne Stretch

ISBN 978-1-5262-0062-4

This is a work of fiction. Names, characters, places and events are used in a fictitious manner. All proceeds from the sale of this book will go towards Teenage Cancer Trust. The opinions in this book may not reflect those of the charity, its staff or current oncology practices. For more information visit www.teenagecancertrust.org

Printed and bound by Stanbury Chameleon, D23, Heritage Business Park, Gosport, Hampshire. PO12 4BG

acknowledgments

Firstly, to my ever-supportive husband, Andrew for 'putting up with me' during the time it has taken to write my book. Andrew has been a bit like Princess Diana when she said there were 'three in her marriage.' We have had three in our marriage for the last few years…Lynne, Andrew and Gwenny, the main character in *Miskin Girl.*

'Thank Andrew for ALL your help and most importantly…being my final proof reader and editor!'

Secondly, I would like to thank my beautiful, intelligent and very loyal daughter, Erica. I would never have got through the M.A. in Creative Writing without Erica. She has not only been my chief reader, but she has helped me with all my assignments and listened to all my *crazy* story ideas. She has continually encouraged me by saying *'You can do it… Lynneeeeee!'*

'I have done it Erica, and it's thanks to you! Thank you for believing in me when I didn't even believe in myself!'

Next, I would like to thank my amazing ninety-year old, mother for constantly giving me the material for my writing. In other words, for sharing her life story of growing up in Seven Sisters. Mams is thrilled that I have used 'fragments' of her stories in this book. I would also like to add an acknowledgement, in memory of my father, Elfryn, who actually owned a printing press when I was growing up.

'Thank you for passing on to me your interest in the printed word. I hope that you would have been proud of me for completing my first novel and for finding a way of putting this story into print.'

Thank you to my brilliantly supportive sisters, Joy and Reena, for allowing me to 'pick their brains' over our childhood experiences. I have used many of our lovely memories as a basis for this book but to stick to assignment guide lines I had to make my story characters more exaggerated in their feelings and actions. Hence, the sisters, friends and the relatives had to be more 'rounded' characters. This meant I had to rethink all my characters and show them as having a 'nastier and meaner' side. I would therefore like to state here that …

'My characters are fictional and their actions do not reflect in any way on my own family and friends.'

Next, I would like to thank Holly Howitt-Dring, my M.A. tutor, at Portsmouth University for tactfully pointing out that I had too many 'nice' characters and for encouraging me to make changes to my protagonist in the first few chapters. Her help and support in writing the first part of my book was invaluable at the time.

I would also like to say a very big thank you to all my fellow creative writing students, who were the readers of my early chapters. In particular, Amanda Donovan, who never gave up on encouraging me to complete my book. She has been a constant support throughout my writing journey…

'Gwenny 'was born' at the same time as Hetty and I wish you every success with Hetty's book'.

My sincere thanks to my writing friend, Kerry Mcphail, for reading parts of my book and helping to write the synopsis…

'You are an inspirational person Kerry. It was thanks to your 'goal posting' that made me finally complete my book. It has been a privilege to be part of your writing group.'

Thank you to Rob and Chris Richardson for inviting me to read my stories at *Rosie's* and to Chris for her eagle-eyed proof reading…

'Thank you for always encouraging me with my writing and for all your support.'

My heartfelt thanks to my very talented friend, Helen Evans, who has spent many hours designing the book cover and working on the illustrations…

'You have interpreted all my thoughts so well Helen. Thank you for being a brilliant artist and giving your time so generously.'

Thank you to my friends Rebecca, Denise, Gill, Lorraine, Louise, Thelma and the two Sheilas for patiently listening and allowing me to 'witter on and on' about my book. Also, to ALL my friends, there is not enough room to list everyone by name, but I would like to say…

'You are all my stars…thank you for being there for me!'

Further thanks go to Beth Bartlam, Teenage Cancer Trust and Kevin Light, Stanbury /Chameleon printers and to all the businesses and individuals, who have helped me raise the money for the printing costs. (A list is printed at the back of this book.)

Finally, thanks to all my contacts at Southampton General Hospital, especially the older children and teenagers, who I met during my son's cancer treatment. My lengthy conversations with these young people inspired me to write *Miskin Girl* and to raise funds for the Teenage Cancer Trust at Southampton.

dEDICAtION

I dedicate this book in memory of our brave and very loving son…

Lawrence James Stretch

Laurie constantly amazed us with the courage he showed when undergoing cancer treatment. He never gave up his fight and was an inspiration to us all.

Laurie was a happy, clever little boy, who was interested in books, cars and trains. He was always setting himself the next challenge, and finding new things that he wanted to achieve in life. He showed us how to live life to the full and never allowed his illness to stop him from doing anything. He was the instigator of our 'family hugs' and taught the 'three of us' everything we know about 'unconditional' love.

'There's no vocabulary for love within a family,
Love that's lived in
But not looked at,
Love within the light of which
All else is seen,
The love within which
All other love finds speech.
This love is silent.'

T. S. Elliot

'Cancer is so limited

It cannot cripple love,

It cannot shatter hope,

It cannot destroy confidence,

It cannot kill friendship,

It cannot silence courage.'

Robert. L. Lynn

cHAPTER oNE - 'sCARED bABY , sCARED bABY'

mISKIN hOUSE, sEVEN sISTERS (1965)

'Scared baby, scared baby, go back to bed. Too scared to go in the printing shed,' her sisters had chanted.

She approached the shed hesitantly. She could hear the muffled sound of a machine. She checked around her. There was no one in sight. Should she? Would she? Could she? Her heart was booming out of her chest. Her hands were trembling and she was beginning to panic…but she heard those mocking voices in her head.

'You… you'll never be brave enough to go inside the printing shed,' her sisters had jeered.

But she was going to prove them wrong. She had seen her father leaving the shed. Now was her chance. He hadn't taken the key. She crept forward, as if it was some kind of trap. She held out her fingers and twisted the hard, wooden door handle in her hand. It turned easily and the door creaked open. Her father would probably be back any minute so she had to move quickly.

She took another step forward and pushed the door. It opened a little and she was immediately greeted by the deafening sound of a working machine. She wrinkled her nose as the smells of oil and printing inks flooded her senses. The new printing press, her father's pride and joy, had arrived a few weeks ago. Her father and her uncle had spent hours trying to get it into the shed, putting it all together and trying it out. Then she remembered Dad's warning words at the breakfast table the other morning, 'On no account must you go into the printing shed, it's too dangerous,' he cautioned his children.

'Where will we keep our bikes?' Beth, her older sister, had asked.

'I've made some room in the wood shed at the bottom of the garden,' answered their father. 'So from now on the printing shed is out of bounds.'

She only wanted one little peep, she would be ever so quick, just in and out, no one would even notice. One tiny peep was all she needed so that she could tell her sisters that she had seen the printing press before they had. With these thoughts in her head, she gave the door a final push.

The big black machine loomed in front of her, unfamiliar and cumbersome, its frame filling the space in the old, wooden shed. An electric light dangled from the dusty beam that ran across the roof space, the bulb enclosed in a homemade brown paper shade, stained and ragged, hung over the machine. The bright light shone directly down into the huge contraption. Intrigued, she stepped nearer, trying to see inside the rollers. She was just stretching up on her tip toes when her foot slipped on an oily patch. She overbalanced and fell towards the clattering noise. She put her hand out to break her fall and somehow got her finger jammed in one of the glistening, greasy 'V' joints. In panic, she screamed, 'Dad…Dad…my finger…my finger!'

She screamed again trying to make her voice heard above the deafening noise of the press.

'Dad!'

Just then a large hand reached out to her, as the machine droned to a halt. She froze in terror as she suddenly realised it was her father, who had switched off the machine. The shed fell into an eerie, unnatural silence as her father's angry face glared down at her. He growled through gritted teeth, 'Don't you ever listen, Gwenny? I've told you a thousand times, you don't come into this shed!'

Gwenny was aware of her father's firm grip on her hand as he slowly and carefully began to release her finger from the machine. There was a lot of blood, but she managed to avert her eyes while he tore the rag from around his waist and quickly stemmed the flow of blood. Then, holding the rag tightly in place, he lifted her arm and held it up above her head.

'What have I told you Gwenny?' he demanded. 'Never go near the printing press, and then I go and catch you with your finger in the machine.'

Gwenny burst out crying. She hated her father being cross with her, 'I'm so sorry Dad… sooooo sorry. I won't do it again I promise.'

'We'd better get you inside. Mum will be wondering what all this noise is about.'

Scooped up in his arms, she was carried up the short path to the house.

'What's happened?' asked Gwenny's mum, placing the baby in his wooden crib.

'I jammed my finger in the printing press,' sniffed Gwenny. Fresh tears trickled down her face, at the sight her mother's concerned expression.

'Do you think she'll have to have stitches?'

'Better let the doctor decide that,' replied Gwenny's father in a low tone. 'Just put a coat over her and I'll carry her up to the surgery now.'

'It'll be closed, it's gone six.'

'Then we'll have to knock loudly. This is an emergency. There's no way we'll get a bus to the hospital at this time of day.'

'Ok, you know best. I'll get Clemmie to come in and look after the little ones.'

'You'd better make it quick as you can… someone will have to hold her if she's got to have stitches.'

'Ok Moc, but not so loud,' Mum replied. 'You'll frighten the life out of Gwenny bach.'

As Gwenny's father carried her in his arms to the doctor's house, she could feel the chill of the wind on her face. She knew her father was angry, but he would take care of her now. An icy blast blew her hair over her face, sticking strands of her golden curls to the wet tears on her cheeks. She hated the cold so she tucked her head into her father's chest. She grew calmer as she breathed in the familiar smell of his oily overalls.

'Dad, I'm scared,' she whispered.

'It's going to be alright,' he reassured her.

Sat on the long wooden bench in the doctor's surgery, Gwenny's body shivered. There was no heating as the coal fires had long gone out.

'So what have you been doing young lady?' asked Doctor Williams, his large hands trying to examine the damaged finger without hurting Gwenny.

He looked at the father, 'Are you sure you wouldn't prefer to go to the hospital?'

Gwenny's father shook his head, so Doctor Williams washed his hands and rolled up his sleeves. Gwenny looked aghast as he prepared the needles.

'Da… Daaaad,' she began to stutter, but as she did so she heard a dull thud behind her. She clenched her body tightly as she turned her head and looked in astonishment. The big bulky body of her father lay on the floor; he had passed out just as Gwenny's mum had walked in through the door.

cHAPTER tWO - gOLDFIsH bOWL

cHILDREN'S cANCER wARD, sOUTHAMPTON (1976)

That memory of her big, strong father passing out on the floor had always made Gwenny smile. She smiled now at the memory of her mum's voice telling the doctor, 'He never could look at a needle.'

He still can't, Gwenny thought to herself; her mum was always the one who flushed out her Hickman line. Gwenny took out her journal and began writing.

Thursday, January 22 (9.00 a.m.)

I'm sitting here feeling like I'm in a goldfish bowl. I've no privacy at all and even if I draw the curtains, the nurses wake me up by taking my temperature or changing my bag of chemo. Don't they realise what it's like for me? I can't get any proper rest. I can't even decide when I put the lights out and go to sleep. I can't wait to go home to my own little bedroom again. Oops, I nearly caught sight of my reflection in the glass then. I try not to look in the window because I just don't recognise myself anymore. Who is this bag of bones staring back at me? My mum, bless her soul, has given up trying to convince me to get a wig for when my hair falls out. God, the ones I've tried already are so itchy. I hate them all. The only thing a wig will be any good for is on the day I walk out of this place! Anyway, who needs a wig when you're stuck in an isolation ward for FIVE more weeks?

10.00 a.m. (After two anti-sickness tablets) - I hate it here, on the ward, with all these little kids. It shouldn't be like this. There should be a separate ward for us bigger kids. It's all so horrid when I throw up in one of those the round cardboard bowls with the whole world staring at me. The doctor has prescribed an anti-sickness drug for me, but it doesn't work! Well, it hasn't worked for me so far! Also, it's not only the kids that look in, but their parents too, who pretty much live on the ward. It's like Swansea market in here some days. There are mothers and fathers everywhere and they often bring the babies in too. Is there really no one they can leave them with? You would think they would have some visiting hours here, but no, the parents of the kids on this ward never go home.

Last night, I woke up in the middle of the night feeling sick and what did I see? One of the newer mums was sitting in the day ward. She was surrounded by other peoples' children throwing up all around her while the nurses changed their beds. Her kid was fast asleep and she should have been too, but there's absolutely nowhere for these parents to sleep. They are lucky if they get a put up bed, and that's only if the nurses have time to get one out. Sometimes, the parents just sleep on the sofas in the children's schoolroom because there is simply nowhere else to go. Thank God I don't need my mum in the middle of the night. It's lovely to have her here in the day though. She's good company, but she doesn't half get on my nerves with all her fussing. It's bad enough that we have to be in here at all, let alone putting up with all the noise. I reckon these walls are paper thin. Last night, I heard the new little boy, Ahmed, crying himself to sleep. None of the nurses could tell if he was in pain because he can't speak English. God, it's ten o'clock already and the doctors will be doing their rounds soon. I hope they're not coming in here today. It's all a bit of a drama when they visit; the doctors have to put their protective suits on. Even the consultant has to put one of those green gowns on. My mum wears them all the time when she visits me. I've forgotten what it's like to see my mum in real clothes.

11.00 a.m. - The doctors have been and gone. Dr Neville asked me if I needed anything and I said, 'Yes, I do, I need to move my bed nearer to the window.'

'No problem,' he answered, so now I can look out on the car park, instead of just into

the ward. If I sit back, I can even see where my mum parks the car without getting out of bed. She has huge problems with parking. The other day when I was standing by the window, I saw her hit the wing mirror of the car next to hers. She thinks I don't know, but I saw it with the binoculars that I borrowed from Clemmie. I can also see the traffic warden prowling the roads around the hospital from up here. I have watched him write out parking tickets every day for a week now. I can't believe it but he actually has a smile on his face when he's making out the tickets. What a weird way to get your kicks; making other people so unhappy and giving them parking fines when they have to visit the hospital. The people I feel sorry for are the genuine cases, the ones who have been stuck in the waiting rooms for hours; then, when they arrive back at their car, you can see by their faces how upset they are as they open the envelope that's been stuck on the windscreen. Not funny!

1.00 p.m. - Today is a good day. I recognised the lunch for a change. It was chicken curry... I could even smell it from in here. It was stone cold, of course, but no one here cares because half the children are too sick to eat, so the parents scoff all the food. It saves them money in the long run because then they don't have to go to the staff canteen. My mum hates going there, she says she would rather eat with me, but of course she can't; my food has to be germ free because I'm, what's known as, neutropenic.

Oh, my flipping cancer has got a hell of a lot to answer for. I hate school, I really do, but sometimes even school seems more appealing than being shut up in here. Some days I feel like I can't even breathe properly. I long to feel the cool, fresh air and the wind blowing through my hair... I know it would be so good. God, that line was almost poetic. I think I can feel another poem coming into my head. I must have written hundreds of poems now. I can't wait to share my new poems with Jackie, she is so much fun and she really believes I've got some talent. She spends all our Maths lesson time on English. I like Jackie, she's a good teacher is Jackie. I wish the teachers in our school were more like her. Hey, I've just realised that there is something positive about being in hospital; I get to read all the books I want and I get to write poems until they are coming out of my ears. I just have to get them printed now. Jackie is going to ask the other children on the ward if they would like to draw some pictures for my book of poems. We are going to print it and then sell copies of the book to raise funds for teenagers with cancer. It's an ambitious plan I know, but Jackie says you have to aim high.

4.00 p.m. - The fire alarm just went off a few minutes ago and I had visions of being stranded as everyone left the building and forgot all about me. As I am the only one stuck in isolation, I expect I'd be the last one taken out. All the little kids were screaming and the mothers were running around like headless chickens. Then the ward manager yelled, 'False alarm!' He was smiling and I heard him saying to one of the nurses that little Ahmed's mother couldn't read the English instructions on the microwave. Apparently, when she was reheating Ahmed's food, she turned the grill on by mistake and set off the smoke alarm. Oh, well, just another day in the goldfish bowl.

Gwenny opened her special book to lock her diary. It had a tiny padlock attached to the cover and as she fiddled with the lock, a piece of folded paper fell out. She picked it up and opened it. It was dated 1967. She read the childish writing…

My vurs

my dad has got a printin pres. he keepz it in the shed.

one day he will lurn to use it. and his fase wont be so red.

by Gwendoline Ann Evans age 5 and a bit

Under the verse printed in a large letters were the words:

my dad is mad.

he can not get the printin press to work.

he has not printed one thing propurle yet and we had it 4 weecs now

cHAPTER tHREE - 'wRONG sPELLING'

mISKIN hOUSE (1965)

Gwenny's father was in a bad mood. He could not get the printing press to work. Gwenny watched as he stomped off to get his bike from the shed.

'Hey, Moc,' Clemmie called after him. 'You go down to Neath for your printing lessons. Gwenny and I will sort out the flyers.'

A few hours after Moc had left to go to the printer's shop, Clemmie and Gwenny were walking through the village, having delivered all the flyers.

'Clemmie,' said Gwenny, in a serious tone. 'Why is Dad always so cross with me?'

'He's not cross with you, Cariad,' replied Clemmie. 'He's just frustrated with himself because he's working too hard. I'm going to help him with the printing business this weekend and together we'll fix the problem.'

He smiled at her reassuringly, 'Meanwhile, you, little lady, should be proud of your dad. He's doing a day shift down the mine. Then he's coming home, having a bath and going straight to town to learn how to use the press. No wonder he's a bit fractious.'

'Why don't you work down the coal mine anymore?' asked Gwenny.

'I've worked there all my life,' replied Clemmie, 'I've got a bad chest these days and it means that I can't go underground anymore.'

'But you still work in the garden and you still look after the hens, don't you?'

'Yes, let's go and get the hens in. You can see if they've laid any eggs for tea.'

'Do I have to touch the eggs?'

'No, but you can help me count how many the eggs the hens have laid.'

'Clemmie, after we've finished counting the eggs, can we look in the printing shed? Dad has gone for his printing lesson and Mum says he won't be back till late.'

'I hope he's taken a light for that bike. He'll do anything...even cycle back in the dark... just to get that printing press working.'

'So Clemmie, please can we go and have a look at the printing press?'

'Okay Gwenny, but you'll have to be careful not to touch anything. Remember what happened last time!'

They both smiled and nodded.

'Clemmie, why have you got black nails?'

'I've been working too long down that coal mine, my little princess. Now enough of your questions and I'll take you to the printing shed. One day, Gwenny, when you're a famous poet, we'll print your book of poems on our very own printing press.'

'Can you print the one I wrote about the sea?'

'Yes, but tell me it again.'

'It's my favourite,' she whispered. 'It's the one I wrote when you took me to Mumbles and we played on the beach and swam in the sea, and when I got home I wrote it in my book because the words were just tumbling out of my head.'

'Oh, Gwenny, my girl, YOU are going to go far in life.'

'No Clemmie, I'm not going far. I'm always going to be your girl and stay right here with you.' He smiled and bending down; he hugged her tightly.

'Clemmie, I love you,' she whispered gently in his ear, and she slipped her small hand into his large hand; the hand with the blackened nails.

Gwenny and her older sister, Beth, were walking home from school. It was a

Wednesday. Gwenny knew that it was a Wednesday because Beth was going to her piano lesson. As soon as they got to the top of their road, Beth threw her satchel at Gwenny.

'Here, Gwenny the wenny,' called Beth, in a silly voice. 'See if you can catch this. I'm going to my music lesson and I'm late already, so catch.'

The satchel fell to the ground as it always did, but Beth didn't bother to turn around. She just ran off to her piano teacher's house with her music book flapping in her hand. Gwenny picked up the satchel and walked down the lane, but as she approached her house she saw two strangers standing on the front doorstep. No one ever used the front door; they didn't need to, as the back door was always open. Gwenny waited by the garden wall and listened to what they were saying. *Oh no,* she thought to herself, *they're the first customers.* She'd heard her parents talking about them, and now they were here, but on a Wednesday. Gwenny was not happy. Wednesday was the only day of the week when she had her mum all to herself. On Wednesday, the little ones were always having their afternoon nap and Beth was at her piano lesson. How dare these people ruin her day? This week Mum had even promised that she would read her new poems with her, and now it was all spoilt. She would have to wait a whole week to have her time with Mum again. It wasn't fair, it simply wasn't fair. But, recognising that she couldn't do anything about it, Gwenny walked down the garden path, opened the back door and dragged the two satchels into the house. Mum was in the kitchen making tea.

'Had a good day at school, Gwenny?' asked Mum, kissing her on her forehead. Then, without waiting for an answer, she poured the hot water into the big, brown teapot and replaced the knitted tea cosy.

'Put your shoes in the cupboard and get your slippers on; we're having tea in the front room. The first customers are here to look at Dad's wedding invitations.'

Tea in the front room…the parlour! No one ever went in the parlour unless it was Christmas or when Beth was practicing her piano. She frowned and reluctantly followed.

'Sit on the pouffe and be a good girl,' whispered Mum.

The couple Gwenny had seen on the door step were sitting side-by-side on the settee. They were flicking through the pages of the 'Invitations' catalogue. Gwenny had been through that book a hundred times choosing the type of print she wanted for her book of poems. Clemmie was always promising he would print her poems when she grew up.

'You'll be the most famous poet in the whole world,' he would say as they read a new poem together, and she would laugh. But she didn't want to be a good girl today; she wanted these people to go home so she could have her mum all to herself.

She listened to Dad's voice as it droned on and on. Gwenny was bored; she began thinking that the young couple would never go home. What could she do to get out of this room? She wasn't allowed in the living room on her own because there was an open fire, and the little ones were asleep upstairs. She couldn't even go out to play in the garden as it was now raining. She sat there and swung back on the pouffe. As she did this, she realised that if she swung back far enough, she would just about be able to reach her milk. Mum had put her glass of milk at the end of the coffee table. Slowly, she slid the pouffe backwards across the linoleum. She had to do it gradually so that no one would notice.

'Keep still, Gwenny,' said Mum, in a slightly annoyed tone.

So Gwenny sat still and began thinking again. What could she do to get her parents to send her out of the room? She could wet herself, but that would be too embarrassing. It had to be something that would work instantly because she didn't want to sit here a minute longer. Then, she had an idea;

'Mum, I think I'm going to be sick.'

She dived off her seat, rushed from the front room, straight over to the kitchen sink and pretended to vomit. Mum apologised to the visitors and followed Gwenny.

'Oh, you poor love,' she said. 'You had better go to your room. If the little ones wake up, they'll have to play in their cots. I'll get you a towel and a sick bowl.'

Gwenny went upstairs to her bedroom, but as soon as her mother had left the room, she got out her little red book and started to write a new poem about the strangers downstairs.

today the stranjurs came to us

we sat in the parlur.

wot a fus.

and now Mum and me have no tim at all.

and I am fed up of bein so smol.

After half an hour, she heard the visitors leave and she quickly put the book away as her mum came into the bedroom.

'How are you feeling love? Have you been sick?'

'No, Mum. Can I have my cawl now?'

'You can't go eating greasy cawl if you have a tummy upset. Come downstairs and bring your pyjamas. I'll warm them in front of the fire.'

Just then, Dad came into the living room to ask Mum to check the spelling on the sample invitation. Mum was busy feeding the baby his mashed up dinner, but Dad insisted she check it there and then.

'Take five minutes, will you Moc?' said Mum, 'Your dinner's in the oven and it will be all dried up if you don't eat it now.'

'It'll be fine. I'll eat later. I want to crack on to get my first order ready for tomorrow. It'll be a lovely surprise for them if the order is ready. Imagine what they'll say to their friends.'

Mum quickly scanned the invitation. She confirmed the spelling and, after wiping the baby's mouth, she turned to Gwenny, 'How are you feeling now love?'

Gwenny looked up from the book she was reading. Her empty tummy gurgled.

'I'm better now. Can I have something to eat please?'

'I'll make you a piece of toast,' said Mum, walking over to the bread bin to cut a slice of bread. 'Pass me the toasting fork and I'll toast it by the fire.'

The next day, the young couple returned after school, to see the sample invitation. Mum had put the electric fire on in the front room again and the whole family sat down to watch the young couple's faces as one of the invitation cards was passed to them for approval. The bride to be was thrilled and squealed in delight.

'Oh, Mr Evans,' she cried. 'The invitation is perfect. I love the gold edging …thank you so much. We must pay you for the order.'

She opened the clip on her handbag to take out her purse, but just as she was going to hand over the money, her fiancé held out the invitation and pointed to the print. Gwenny watched her father's face. It was beaming, but the moment was short lived when the young man, looking embarrassed and red faced, suddenly blurted out,

'I'm afraid we can't accept this invitation. It's got the wrong spelling of *thier*.'

Dad looked up in amazement and snatched the invitation card from the young man's hand. He read:

Mr and Mrs Jones request the pleasure of

………………………………………………………………………………

at the wedding of thier daughter…

Gwenny stared at her father, his face had turned white and his eyes looked strained. He knew that it wasn't only the sample copy that was spelt incorrectly, but all the gold rimmed invitations, one hundred in all. They would all have to be reprinted…Ouch!

A few minutes later the young couple left, without the invitations. Dad was silent. Gwenny glanced around the small room, no one dared move. Then, she watched in complete horror as her father sank back in his armchair, put his face in his hands and cried.

cHAPTER fOUR - 'lAUGHTER iS tHE bEsT mEDIcINE'

cHILDREN'S cANCER wARD, sOUTHAMPTON (1976)

Gwenny cried and cried. She cried through the night. She cried through breakfast. She was even crying when the doctors arrived for their daily ward round.

'I want to go home,' moaned Gwenny. 'You can't keep me here against my will. I'm going to die anyway.'

Doctor Neville was so concerned about her crying that he even gowned up and entered Gwenny's isolation room. He prescribed laughter and Gwenny smiled for the first time in twenty four hours.

Friday, January 23 (9.00 a.m.)

I like Doctor Neville. I like him a lot. He told me, 'It's good to laugh' and I believe him. It really is important to laugh because it actually does make me feel better. But when I answered I was honest with him; 'How can I laugh when I feel like I'm living in a fish tank and I'm not allowed out?' But he didn't just turn away. He looked me straight in the eyes and said, 'Gwendoline' (this made me smile because nobody calls me Gwendoline.) 'You like writing don't you? How about writing down all the funny stories that your family and friends have ever told you? And if you can't remember all the details, just make some of it up, like you do with your poems. That should bring a smile to your face, what do you think?'

So, for once in my life, I am going to do what the doctor ordered. I am going to make myself laugh and smile by writing down lots of funny stories in my journal. I think I'll start my Mum, who always has a silly story to tell. She always says that she doesn't know how these things always happen to her. But they do! My only problem is where to start. Ok... I'll start with a title:-

Funny stories to make me laugh (prescribed by Dr Neville)

My mum, she actually went to work... yes, to work... in school as a trainee teacher with ... wait for it... with two different shoes on! Now, everyone's worn two mismatched socks, especially navy and black ones on a dark winter morning, but it wasn't winter...even! And, to be honest, anyone in their right mind would feel a bit lopsided with two different shoes on... wouldn't you? Apparently, not my mum! She even walked to school and didn't bat an eyelid. That was, until Johnny Watson, who sat by her feet in school assembly, asked in his loudest voice, 'Mrs Evans, why have you got two different shoes on?'

My mum said she wished the floor could have devoured her up right there, at that exact moment, on that very spot, in front of the whole school. And worse still, it happened in front of the parents, who had come to watch the assembly. The hushed sniggers went around the room like a never ending wave of sounds until the head teacher had to signal for silence. Meanwhile, my mum...bless her heart... managed to hide her mismatched shoes under her long flared trousers. Then, she used one of her well-rehearsed tactics, she gave her class one of her best ever 'teacher' stares. They didn't dare to laugh after that, well, you wouldn't would you? It wouldn't be polite. But I know that all the parents were trying their best not to stare at my mum's feet as she walked out of the school hall. I know because I was there, it happened when I still used to go to school. That is, before I had this stupid cancer!

Another story that always makes me laugh is about my mum and the white bikini. My mum won a weekend break to Cornwall. Her face was a picture when she found out. I don't think she'd ever been to a posh hotel before. Unfortunately, the hotel hadn't informed her that there was a swimming pool, so she hadn't packed a swimsuit. The only swimwear in the hotel shop was a white bikini, so Mum bought it because she was desperate to use the hotel pool. Mum entered the pool area with her towel wrapped around her and placed it very near the steps into the pool. When she was ready to exit the pool Mum looked down and realised that the bikini had no lining and was completely see-through. She grabbed her towel and made a quick dash for the changing room, but in her hurry she bumped straight into an older man who had just come out of the men's changing room. In the clash, Mum managed to drop her towel and almost gave the pensioner a heart attack. That story is always guaranteed to make everyone laugh. After all, Mum is hardly a teenager and doesn't usually go around displaying so much bare flesh!

The last story isn't really laughable...just funny in a strange way...it's to do with my birth. Mum was due to give birth to me at home, but instead of taking things easy like she should have, she decided to clean out the box room. I mean, who would do that when you're nine months pregnant? While she was moving boxes she felt a pain in her tummy and apparently, so I am told, gave birth to me there and then on the box room floor. The only other people in the house at the time were Clemmie and Beth. So, after making sure I was wrapped safely in my Mum's arms. Clemmie took Beth next door to phone for the midwife. I love hearing the story about my birth. I'm so glad that Clemmie was there to help Mum and me. I think that's why I'm so special to him.

<u>Monday, January 26 (10.00 a.m.)</u>

I could not believe what happened this afternoon. In fact, I was horrified when I saw Miss Pudson, Daisy and Shuff walk into the corridor outside my room. I simply could not believe my eyes...no one from school had ever come to visit before, so I immediately wondered if Dr Neville had something to do with it.

Pudson, who had led them down the corridor, broke the ice by telling me about their journey to the hospital and how they had missed double Maths to visit me. Pudson did most of the talking; she didn't seem to notice the other two shuffling their feet from side-to-side and taking great care to avoid making eye contact with me. Daisy and Shuff were probably nominated by the rest of the class because they were the form prefects. 'False cows,' I thought to myself, remembering what Daisy and her lot had done to me in the toilet on the last day of term.

Pudson prattled on about auditions for the end of term show. She encouraged Daisy to update me on how the hockey team was doing.

'You must come and watch us play when you come home from hospital,' chirped Daisy, with a feigned smile.

For once I was glad of the glass panel between us, but my response was thankfully interrupted by the arrival of a trolley pushed by Harry, one of the hospital porters.

'A large parcel for Miss Gwenny Evans,' Harry shouted in a cheerful voice.

The boxed parcel, all wrapped in brown paper, needed a lot of manoeuvring to get in through the hatch. A gowned nurse had to come into my cubicle to open the interior doors. Harry opened the outer doors under the windowsill and then pushed the box through the hatch. The nurse helped me to put my protective gloves on while I read the card which read:

With our very best wishes

Get well soon

Miss Pudson and all the students in Form 5C

I couldn't wait to tear the paper off, but I started to cry as soon as I saw that it was a fourteen-inch black and white portable telly. It was exactly what I had been longing for, but I was so embarrassed about my tears. As I struggled to control myself and search for a tissue, I heard the nurse explain that the treatment was making me very emotional and that it would be best if the visitors left. I was so relieved.

After they had gone, I thought 'Great, now I can watch "Coronation Street" without missing an episode'. But I must admit... I did have a problem with the gift itself. I wondered whether the bullies had actually contributed to my present? Were they feeling a little bit miffed that the person they had constantly bullied was not around to pick on anymore?

<u>*Tuesday, January 27 (8.30 a.m.)*</u>

Last night I had one of my nightmares about the bullies. In the dream, I was with my younger sister, Rosie and her friend. We were in the local cafe after school when, all of a sudden, I was aware of a voice that I dreaded hearing...then I saw Daisy's reflection in the mirror. I felt sick and grabbed my bag to put my sunglasses on (I don't know why I needed sunglasses in my dream but I remembered that part clearly.) I asked Rosie and her friend to make their way to the exit as quickly as they could. For once, Rosie didn't argue and we just turned around and tried to get out. Unfortunately, a group of first formers were blocking the doorway because it had started raining outside. As a result, no one was going anywhere. Daisy spotted that we were trying to escape so she and her group of friends surrounded me. Then Daisy sneered in a loud voice, 'Who's been doing all her homework then? Who's got an 'A' for her poetry then? What did you have to do Welshy? Did you have to write it in your own stupid language and get it translated?'

Her group responded by laughing so Daisy was encouraged to carry on. I looked across to my sister being pushed by the crowd and indicated to her to be silent as Daisy's taunts continued. 'We're going to get you, aren't we girls? We're going to tear your homework book up and you won't be able to revise for the exams. So you will fail. Ha...ha... teacher's pet, grade 'F'... that would be a laugh.'

She turned to her cronies and they giggled.

'You won't be so bloody perfect then will you? You Welsh git. We don't want your sort "down by yer" do we?'

The group responded once more by mimicking my Welsh accent and I tried to turn away.

'Hey, don't you be so rude, Taff. Don't you dare ignore me.'

Daisy came up behind me and poked me in the back with her finger. I wouldn't turn around. I tried to shrug her hand off as Rosie raised her arm to try to stop Daisy prodding me, but I shook my head. I wasn't going to let my little sister get into trouble because of me. That's where the dream ended, but it does seem the bullies are on my mind all the time, even in my dreams. I remembered all the details of the dream so vividly I had to record it. As I'm writing, I'm finding it really hard because it is dragging up what I've been through in the last few months. I often think back to what it was like when I first arrived at my new school in England. The bullies had a field day with the way I spoke. They said that they didn't understand my accent and they would ask me to repeat my words and make jokes about my pronunciation. It was embarrassing and it was humiliating, but I put up with it because I thought there was no other choice. They somehow made me feel that I deserved to be treated in that way. I began feeling that I couldn't ever open my mouth because whenever I did there was always a sneering comment. They even scoffed at the poems I read out in class so I stopped writing them. In fact, I put my whole life on hold because of what they were doing to me. They hid my sandwiches. They stole my bus pass. They even wrote anonymous notes that said, 'You talk like crap! Go back to your own country... you Welsh idiot.' I didn't dare tell anyone that I was being picked on because Mum would have worried. That's why I was so shocked that I got the portable television.

I know I am more protected here in hospital. At last, I have found a place where I feel safe. I can read books and I can make up poems whenever I want. It's just a shame that I have to get filled with drugs at the same time!

P.S. I forgot to mention. I really fancy James, the new boy in Day Ward. I've seen him walk past my window a few times. Wonder if he likes girls with very little hair?

cHAPTER fIVE - tHE bUTCHER, tHE bAKER, tHE cANDLESTICK mAKER

mISKIN hOUSE (1966)

'Mum, it's the giant with no hair. He's leaning his bike against our wall,' called Gwenny.

Mum came rushing down the stairs. She held her baby son wrapped tightly in a shawl so she still had her hands free to carry out her jobs.

'Gwenny, don't be silly and stop frightening Rosie. It's only Ifor from the butcher's shop. Have you seen my purse?'

The sisters shook their heads and went back to the window to watch Ifor clumping down the garden path. He gave a cursory knock on the back of the door and walked in, placing the parcel of meat wrapped in newspaper on the scullery table. Gwenny and Rosie peeped from behind the glass door and watched as Ifor took the bill from his pocket. They could hear Mum saying, 'I'm sure I had my purse when Dai Post brought that parcel.'

Then, with a sudden change of mind, Mum headed back upstairs.

'I had it when I was changing the beds and I must have left it on the ottoman.'

She hurried back to the scullery a few minutes later.

'Sorry to keep you waiting Ifor,' said Mum, counting out the coins and adding some extra pennies. 'Did you have everything that I ordered last week?'

'Ye... ye...ssss, Mrs Evan...sss,' he stuttered as he shuffled from one foot to another.

Gwenny always thought that Ifor looked like an over-grown schoolboy. He wore trousers that were too short for his long legs and boots that were far too big for his large feet. Mum offered him a drink of homemade lemonade, and as he drunk it he stared at the girls, and they in turn stared back. They didn't mean to be rude but they weren't used to seeing men as tall as Ifor in their small scullery. In fact, Gwenny and Rosie were a little in awe of Ifor. They were a very cautious pair without their big sister around, but Beth was always helping Dad when Ifor delivered the meat order.

'Bye Mrs Evans,' said Ifor. 'Thank you for the drink of lemonade.'

Gwenny returned to the window seat, followed by Rosie. Gwenny shivered, she hated the sound of Ifor's voice. It frightened her that such a giant of a man should have such a childlike voice.

'Oh dear, where's my list for next week? I think I put it on the pantry shelf.' said Mum. She opened the pantry door and picked up a torn envelope. She handed it to Ifor.

'Now Ifor, don't forget that I like lean bacon...and pork sausages, not beef.'

Ifor nodded.

'And you will remember to give next week's list to your uncle, won't you?'

'I won't forget, Mrs Evans,' promised Ifor, pocketing the list. Then, he opened the back door and negotiated the steps down to the path.

'Take care Ifor. See you next Friday.'

Then Mum turned to the girls, 'I'm just going to put the baby in his pram out the front. Can you start unpacking the meat and put it on the cold slab in the pantry? Then we'll have to write the list for Mr Baker. He should be here with our groceries any minute.'

A few moments later Gwenny and Rosie sat side by side on the rag mats, which Mum had made. The rag mats were a welcome addition to the pantry as the floor was made of flagstones which were always very cold to sit on. Meanwhile, Mum stood behind the girls and scanned the pantry shelves. She started writing her list on the back of a torn envelope:-

2lb of sugar

1 dozen eggs

1 packet of suet

½ lb salt butter

3lb plain flour

2 large tins of baked beans

2 tins of tomato soup

Meanwhile, Gwenny had found another envelope to make her own list. She chewed the end of her pencil and then asked two year old Rosie, 'What shall we write on our list? Shall we put sherbet?'

'Th…sw… eeties,' answered Rosie.

Gwenny wrote in her best writing:

shwetz

shurbit

lolepops

'Okay Rosie, I've finished,' said Gwenny. 'When Mum is busy we'll put our list in the empty box. Mr Baker will read it and put the sherbet, sweets and lollipops in our box for next week.'

'Th…swwee…eeties… next week,' repeated Rosie, with a lisp.

Just then there was a knock on the back door.

'Gwenny, please go and open the door for Mr Baker,' called Mum.

Gwenny got up and walked to the back door. She turned the door knob. 'Hello,' she said, but stepped back in fright as she saw Mr Baker struggling to remain upright. He was clutching the box of groceries to his chest. Gwenny's eyes were

were drawn to the way that the eggs swayed on the top of the box.

'Mr Baker, look out… the eggs are falling,' she stammered as she watched his face contort. He seemed to clutch the box even closer to his chest. Then, as if in slow motion, the open tray of eggs started to slip to the floor. Gwenny screamed as the whole box of groceries fell from his arms, the eggshells cracked and the yolks split open as they hit the concrete. The bag of flour spilled its contents and a fine mist of white powder covered Mr Baker's face. He grunted and, clutching the left side of his chest, slumped to the ground. Gwenny heard someone yelling and realised the screams were coming from her own mouth.

'Mum, Mum, come quickly. Mr Baker has fallen down the steps and he's smashed all the eggs!'

cHAPTER sIX – eGGS fOR bREAKFAST

cHILDREN'S cANCER wARD, sOUTHAMPTON (1976)

'Yuk,' screamed Gwenny, 'I've got the wrong breakfast. I've got eggs. I hate eggs.'

The new nurse came rushing back to the hatch, bringing the correct tray with her.

'I'm so sorry,' she apologised.' It's my first day on this ward and I thought you were bed one.'

'But I'm neutropenic,' insisted Gwenny, through the window. 'I shouldn't even have eggs unless they are well cooked.'

'Sorry. I'm so sorry. Please don't tell Sister or I'll...'

'What's that? What's wrong Gwenny?' interrupted the ward sister.

'Oh, sorry Sister, it was my fault. I gave the breakfast tray for bed one to bed ten by mistake.'

'Well... Nurse... I think you had better take a break. I'll need to speak to you when you return. We can't afford to make mistakes like that on this ward.'

The nurse walked away with tears in her eyes. Gwenny felt ashamed of herself for making such a fuss, but she really did hate eggs. She hoped she would be able to talk to Sister later to try to explain that it was an easy mistake for the young nurse to make.

Wednesday, January 28 (8.00 a.m.)

James, the new boy, is a day patient on our ward today. He is very good looking, BUT he hasn't even glanced my way so far! I can completely understand why he is looking so miserable. I can remember vividly how I felt on my first day on the ward. I felt like a 'ghost' doing a 'death' walk. I was really scared as I didn't know what to expect. I had visions of having to stay all alone in hospital, but of course it's nothing like you imagine. Everyone is so kind here. Since my first day I have witnessed so many children arrive on the ward. There are new faces every week. It's a completely new world to them, but it's the only one I know right now. I've just decided that I'm going to make a note each time James passes my window. Well, I have nothing better to do with my time today!

8.47 a.m. - James walked pass with a nurse. She took his temperature and his blood pressure. Then, she noted his weight and attempted to measure his height. But there was a slight problem. He was so tall he went right off the top of the chart and so the nurse had to stand on a stool and mark the wall. He made the nurse laugh with his banter... I can tell he is going to be a joker. When he walked back up the corridor I pretended to be fiddling with my curtains so that I could get a good look. I love the way he strides pass my room. He is so lanky and slim. I love the way he wears a denim shirt and matching denim jeans. He also wears a gold chain and a leather belt. I love gold chains and leather belts. I love everything about him. I wonder how old he is... I must ask Jackie tomorrow. I wonder what star sign he is. I'm keeping my fingers crossed he is Capricorn. According to Rhiannon, my cousin who loves reading horoscopes and knows everything about star signs, I am most compatible with Capricorns. He must be a Capricorn... how can I find out?

10.08 a.m. - James walked past my room with his mum. They were going to get his bloods done at the blood department downstairs. I know that because they always give you a plastic bag with all the forms inside and I saw his mum was carrying the exact one I used to get. I couldn't help noticing how he towers over his mum. He must take after his Dad. I wonder if he has any brothers or sisters...Mum had to bring

Rosie and Gareth with us on my first visit, but they didn't come again after that first time. I love the way he combs his hair to the side. I wonder if he knows that the treatment makes your hair fall out. He has tanned skin even in the winter perhaps he has been skiing? He is so good looking.

10.45 a.m. – James walked back to his room with his mum again. There must have been a queue in the blood department today... it never usually takes that long. Now they will have to wait on the ward for the results. The waiting around in this place is awful. I saw James carrying a magazine called 'Sailing.' He must be interested in boats. Hence... his tanned skin! What a shame I know nothing about boats! N.B. Find out about boats!!!!

11.48 a.m. – James walked past alone. He was holding a paper bag. I expect it was his lunch as the children on the day ward never get offered any lunch. He's allowed to eat in the school room. Jackie always finds something for the day patients to do... even if it's just a sketch pad.

3.05 p.m. - James and his mum went past. I wonder if he's going home. His mum smiled at me on the way out. She smiled in that way people do when they feel sorry for you. They start to curl their lips but they don't know if they should smile or not. I've seen that type of smile so many times since I've been ill.

3.32 p.m. - James came back to the ward alone. He was carrying a see - through bag with white boxes. I bet he's got all his 'meds' to take home. I heard him say to the day ward manager, 'I'll see you tomorrow.' Yippee! I get to see James again tomorrow.

Thursday, January 29 (8.35 a.m.)

James must have arrived very early on the ward this morning. When I saw him he was already wearing a navy blue dressing gown with a theatre gown underneath. He was going to the theatre with the hospital porter who usually makes the younger kids sit in the wheelchair. His mum was walking behind. She looked as if she had been crying. He's probably going to have an exploratory operation. It doesn't take them long to do the actual procedure but it is the anaesthetic that's always the problem, or so Dr Neville told me. I am like a little 'expert' when it comes to my treatment because I won't let anyone do anything to me until I have found out what they are going to do and why. I know every stage of my chemotherapy plan as I've read the leaflet from cover to cover several times. My mum says I will end up having all the side effects because I know them so well. I wish James would make eye contact with me. He did glance my way for a few seconds, but I was so scared that he would see that I fancy him that I turned away. I am really mad with myself. He is my perfect match as a boyfriend. I need to do something that will make him notice me. I might even take off my itchy wig. Then... he will have something to stare at!

10.00 a.m. - James came past lying on a trolley. His mum was walking beside him holding his hand. He didn't look too great. He had one of those injection things in the back of his hand. All the nurses say, 'This is not going to hurt', but I don't listen to them anymore...they are all fibbers because it hurts like hell. James has all my sympathy. I must tell Jackie that I'm willing to talk to him about the treatment. I'm going to pray that he'll recover quickly from the anaesthetic.

I'm really cheesed off! I've sat in this room alone all day. I can hardly wait for Mum to come after tea. It breaks the day up having a visitor at tea time. I think I've done enough writing for one day...I'm going to get on with my jigsaw now. I did a five hundred piece jigsaw last week and this week I've started my new jigsaw with one thousand pieces. I am using the table that you have your meals on because there is simply nowhere else to put such a big jigsaw. It's great because I can leave it out and go back to it whenever I want. I absolutely love puzzles!

cHAPTER sEVEN - gOOD lITTLE wORKER

mISKIN hOUSE (1967)

Gwenny loved jigsaw puzzles. She was sitting at the table with Clemmie and he was trying to help her find the straight edge pieces to start her jigsaw. She was waiting for her dad to return home after refereeing a local football match.

'Dad, can I help you in the printing shed today? Pleeeeeease?' pleaded Gwenny as soon as her father opened the back door,

Dad looked at Gwenny. She asked the same question at least once every day and he always refused, but she didn't ever give up.

'Moc, for goodness sake, give her a little job to do in the printing shed.' encouraged Clemmie. 'She's six years old now. She won't go poking her fingers into things like she used to. Give her a chance to prove she can help you.'

'Okay,' said Dad reluctantly. 'Go and put an apron on and I'll see you in the printing shed in ten minutes.'

Gwenny was elated and began to sing the alphabet song as she went to fetch her apron.

'A B C D E F G H I J K L M N O P Q R S T U V W X Y Z', she chanted.

Gwenny knew her alphabet because she practised it every night before she went to bed. It was because she knew her alphabet so well that her dad had agreed to her helping in the printing shed this afternoon. She knew it would take Dad a long time to put a new template together on his own and she could help him find all the letters. It was always a tricky job because the letters had to be selected in reverse so that they came out right way around but Gwenny enjoyed the challenge!

'Now Gwenny, listen carefully,' ordered Dad in a solemn voice. 'You have to find ALL these letters and you have to place them in the correct order or this won't work. If you miss out just one letter the typesetting could be wrong.'

'I'll be very careful Dad,' promised Gwenny.

'Now I've written down the first line that you need to set up and as you find each letter I want you to place it in the wooden tray. I also need you to tick it off on this piece of paper so that we know we've got the right letters. When you've found all the letters, I'll check them and then we'll put it on the press.'

'Dad, has Beth helped you in the shed?'

'No Gwenny. She's too busy doing her homework, so that she can pass the eleven plus and go to the grammar school.'

'Am I going to grammar school too?'

'I should hope so.'

'But Dad, what if I don't pass the eleven plus?'

'You will pass,' growled Dad. 'There's no way a daughter of mine is not going to pass the eleven plus.'

'Dad,' asked Gwenny, a few minutes later. 'Why aren't there more letters in the alphabet?'

'Don't know, Gwenny.'

'But there are lots more letters in the Welsh alphabet. We have *ch*, *ll* and *dd*.'

'Yes Gwenny, I know all that, but now it's time to concentrate. So enough of your questions, let's get on with our jobs.'

'Dad, what comes after L? Is it M or N?'

'You know it's M,' grumbled Dad. 'If you can't do the job I'll call Beth to do it, so hurry up now.'

'Nearly finished,' she said as she laid out the letters on the flat ink-stained printing tray, some time later.

'Neath… Boys'… Club… Dance…,' she began to read aloud.

'You've finished the top line then,' remarked Dad, looking over her shoulder.

'Yes, and I checked it twice to make sure.'

'Good girl. Well done. You're a good little worker, you are,' he smiled at her and she returned his smile beaming from ear to ear. It meant everything to her to get that little bit of praise. Gwenny loved her dad dearly but she knew that he had wanted a son when she had been born. It was strange how she felt that she was a big disappointment to him. Where that feeling came from she didn't really know, but as a result she always struggled hard to please her dad; she was so desperate for him to like her. Today, he had praised her and she felt like running to tell her mum. Today Gwenny was Dad's favourite girl!

So the typeset was complete and the first *'Dance'* tickets were being put on the press. Her father always worked quickly once the typeset was ready. He placed each piece of card individually on the machine, the card had to be lined up correctly or the print would come out on a slant. Sometimes, it took her dad all night to finish an order, and then the Watkins family, who lived next door, would complain loudly from behind the tall hedge. They said that they couldn't sleep a wink because of the noise coming from the printing shed. Gwenny's mum was mortified when she and Gwenny happened to eavesdrop on Mrs Watkins talking to the vicar.

'We have to put up with that printing machine rumbling right through the night,' complained Mrs Watkins.

'I know,' said the vicar in a sympathetic tone. 'You've got a lot to put up with living next door to a family with a printing press.'

Gwenny knew that her mum felt bad enough about the noise from the printing press but with Mrs Watkins telling the vicar that Dad had kept them awake all night, Gwenny and Mum knew it would be round the whole street the next day. No one told the vicar anything 'private' because it was common knowledge that his wife was the biggest gossip in the village.

Gwenny and Mum had heard the conversation while they were getting the tin bath ready for bath time. The children always had their baths on Friday nights. They all had their hair washed and were allowed to stay up late until their hair was dry.

Gwenny loved Fridays because they had fish and chips for tea. Beth and Gwenny were sent up the fish shop to get two fish in batter and a pile of chips to share. At the chip shop, Beth asked for the order to be wrapped, but all the way home Gwenny picked at the soggy newspaper. 'I love the taste of hot chips,' said Gwenny, licking her salty fingers.

Beth looked on in disgust, 'I'm going to tell Mum about you pinching the chips. Then you won't have any chips to go with your fish.'

After tea, Beth and Gwenny watched *Blue Peter* and played out in the garden until Mum was ready for bath time. All the water had to be boiled in kettles and big pans and so it took ages for the bath to be the right temperature for the girls' baths. Then, they took turns in climbing into the bath tub in front of the fire and having their long hair washed with carbolic soap.

By the time Gwenny was bathed, Clemmie had arrived. His first job every Friday evening was to towel dry Gwenny's hair. Then he would go through her hair with a fine comb checking for nits. He always made Gwenny laugh when they were doing this.

'Stop wriggling Gwenny, I think I saw the chick.'

Then, Clemmie would click the nails on his fingers together to make a loud sound. Gwenny never knew whether he was teasing or not, but it worked and she remained still until Clemmie had finished checking her hair. As he combed her hair, she would listen to Clemmie singing one of his favourite songs, *We'll Keep a Welcome in the Hillside*, in his deep, contralto voice. His voice filled the room as Gwenny sat on the little wooden milking stool that he had made for her. Gwenny would laugh as he made up new words for songs, 'She has the loveliest hair in the world. It's like a shimmering waterfall… La- La- La- Laaaaaah.'

'Comb my hair again,' pleaded Gwenny, 'I love watching television on Friday nights… it's *Emergency Ward 10* and *Bonanza*.'

Sometimes, Clemmie would call at the cafe and buy them a bar of *Five Boys Chocolate*. Beth always ate her chocolate within a few minutes, while Gwenny savoured every piece of the delicious milk chocolate.

'I hate your hair,' Beth whispered to Gwenny. 'I heard Mum say she's going to cut it off because you're always catching nits. Then you'll look just like a boy.'

'I don't want to look like a boy,' moaned Gwenny.

'And don't you dare tell Mum what I just said, or I'll use the scissors, from my new manicure set, to cut off your plaits when you're asleep,' hissed Beth.

Gwenny shuddered at the thought of having her hair cut, but she knew that she would never tell on Beth. She was much too scared to even think about it. Clemmie finished combing Gwenny's hair just as the familiar theme tune to *Bonanza* filled the room and the family settled down to watch their favourite programme. Mum ran her fingers through Gwenny's hair every few minutes to check that it was drying. Then, she gently pushed Gwenny a little closer to the fire.

'Not many children her age have such thick hair,' Mum observed to Clemmie.

'Yes, she's going to be the envy of her friends with hair like that.'

cHAPTER eIGHT – sNAP, CRACKLE, POP!

cHILDREN'S cANCER wARD, sOUTHAMPTON (1976)

Monday, February 2 (8.30 a.m.)

Today I was only allowed a small sealed packet of cereal because I'm neutropenic. As the breakfast trolley arrived I was surprised that I actually felt like eating; in fact, my stomach was churning with anticipation. It's over a week now since I started taking the anti sickness drugs. Hurrah... I can eat at last without being sick! As I opened the Rice Krispies variety pack box and poured the milk I felt like a little girl again. I remembered how my sisters and I had listened to hear the 'snap, crackle and pop.' I was so excited. I tried to open the milk carton but it took me ages as the bendy straw would not break the hole. Then, just as I put my spoon into the bowl to take my first mouthful, a clump of my hair fell into my cereal bowl and I heard the sound I'd been waiting for 'Snap... crackle... pop!' It put me right off my cereal and I couldn't have anything else as the breakfast trolley had already been taken away.

10.00 a.m. – I've been waiting for over thirty minutes and Dr Neville hasn't even arrived yet. While I was gazing out of the window with my binoculars, I overheard one of the cleaners saying how brave the children on the ward are. It suddenly struck me that I'm one of the children they are talking about, but I don't think of myself as being brave, so I wrote these lines:

Brave girl, brave girl

How many times do I hear those words?

And yet I am not brave at all.

I am full of illness, disease and pain,

I feel I have no choices,

If I want to live I need to have the treatment.

But I do not feel brave,

Inside...I'm still that little child, who always was and still is...a scared baby.

I want to keep these lines as I know they'll be an inspiration for one of my next poems. People always ask what inspires me and I always answer that I don't know because the words just pop into my head at any time of day. When it happens I just have to stop everything and write them down. I have a drawer at home filled with scraps of paper. I even wrote a poem with mum's lipstick once because I couldn't find a pen. She was not amused!

<u>*Tuesday, February 3 (9.30 a.m.)*</u>

I can't get comfy in my bed today. My stomach is bloated, my back aches like hell, I am constipated and very uncomfortable. My mum suggested I get up from bed and sit on a chair instead. I'm beginning to feel like Goldilocks, who tried out all the chairs in the story of the Three Bears. While my mum was re-making my bed, I started trying all the chairs in my room. First, I tried the visitor's chair, but that was too low. Then, I tried the desk chair, but that was too high. Then, I tried the kids' chair and that was just right so I sat there for five minutes until my bottom got a bit sore again. And yes, I was just like Goldilocks in the story except that I haven't any golden hair...instead... I now have 'tufts' of hair. The biggest problem is that wherever I sit, I leave a trail of hair behind me. I'm bit like my cat, Muffin when he's shedding his winter coat. Also, it's a pain trying to go to sleep with hair on my pillow... when I turn the pillow over to the cool side... I suddenly get a mouthful of hair. The last few days I have been on chemo during the day and whenever I move around I have to take my drugs trolley with me. The younger kids have named the chemo trolley 'Robbie Robot'. The nurses let us put stickers on the metal part so we can recognise our own trolley. Some days I can even feel the drugs running through my veins. It's like an icy chill running through my body and I never know when it's suddenly going to make me shiver. The chemo drugs leave a strange metallic taste in my mouth so that everything I eat tastes a bit odd. Last night my chemo started late again, so when I woke up this morning I was still connected up. It's really inconvenient because I have to move carefully, pulling the wheeled trolley, which is attached to my Hickman line behind me. I even have to take my 'Robbie Robot' with me to the toilet and the bathroom! I can't go anywhere without it. I absolutely hate bathing or showering with it and I know that the other children do too. I've seen the little toddlers as they try to slip away from their mums in the bathroom. They're trying to escape from parents who run behind them with towels and wet flannels. I don't blame the kids for trying to get away. I know how awkward it is to get into your bath with a line sticking out of your chest. The new mums will learn they don't have to bathe their kids every day, sometimes just a 'blanket bath' will have to do. Keeping teeth clean and using mouthwash is also a nightmare but again the little ones run away. I wish I could too I hate the taste of the mouthwash they prescribe. They should make it in a nice flavour like strawberry or vanilla…I must ask Doctor Neville about that.

The little ones have to have their exercise time but it's absolutely ridiculous to expect me to do exercises. I would love to swim one hundred lengths every day. Yeah, in my dreams! My excuse is that for the few hours I am disconnected I dash to the window so that I can get a few breaths of fresh air into my lungs. But most of the time I feel absolutely exhausted, so I just sleep and watch the television. It's a vicious circle of no exercise, no eating and lots of sleeping. At the times when I feel creative I just write in my journal or think of lines for my new poems.

Friday, February 6 (9.30 a.m.)

Every Friday the kids on the ward 'do a P.E session' with Jackie in the school room... they love it! They don't seem to have an excuse like me, but they don't have to do the exercises if they don't want to and some of the kids are far too ill. Anyway, Friday is P.E. afternoon and with seven 'Robbie Robots' and seven parents attached to their off spring, the room quickly fills up. P.E. involves sitting on a chair. They all take part as much as possible and work on their co-ordination and ball skills. I went to P.E. the first week I was here so that's how I know what they do, but I am not allowed to take part in P.E. now...I can't mix with the other children. The physiotherapist comes to give me my weekly sessions and...oh, I almost forgot...my reading glasses arrived today. I had to have hearing and sight tests a couple of weeks ago just in case my ears and eyes were being affected by the drugs. My physiotherapist saw me squinting when I was trying to read my chemo bag and now I'm going to have to wear glasses for reading. No hair, bad eyesight and more hearing tests...no hope for me. I do NOT stand a chance with James. I have clumps of hair falling out all the time... I must look like a complete freak.

P.S. I hate the specs! (But I only have to wear them for reading).

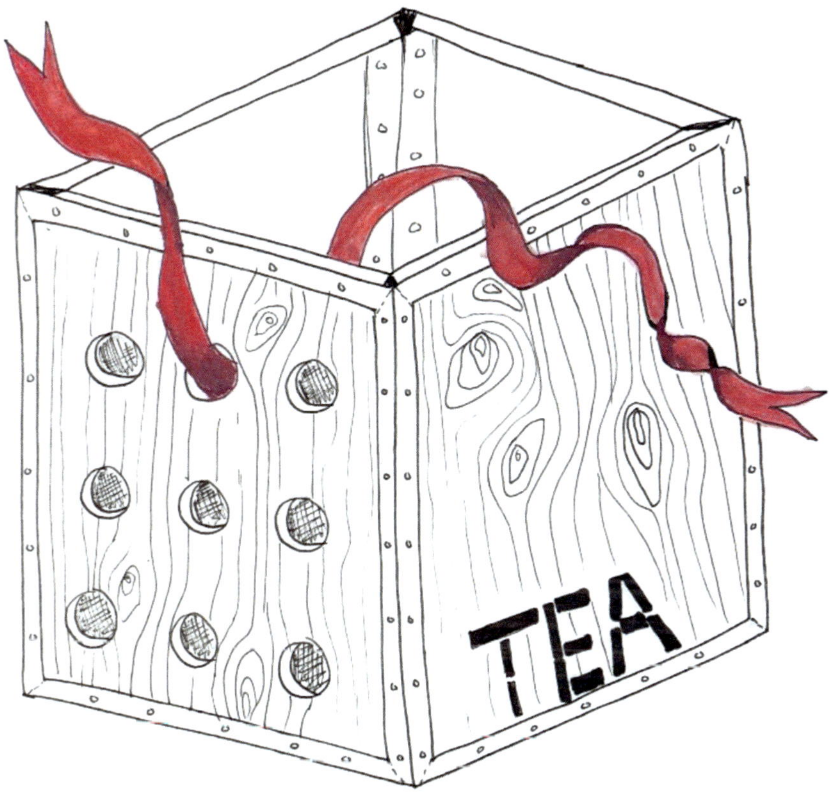
TEA

cHAPTER nINE - iN tHE boX

mISKIN hOUSE (1968)

Gwenny crept across the upstairs landing and hoped the wooden floorboards would not creak. The bedroom door was slightly ajar, and as soon as she entered the room she was greeted with the sound of snoring coming from under the eiderdown.

Good, she thought, *Beth was asleep.*

Her eyes adjusted to the dimness of the room as the curtains swayed slightly in the cool evening breeze. She quickly scanned the furniture to find where Beth had put her glasses. They were on the dressing table next to the bed. Gwenny hesitated and looked across the rose-patterned linoleum. Then, she tiptoed across the room keeping her eyes firmly fixed on the sleeping figure in the bed.

Gwenny knew that if she was caught in her sister's bedroom there would be ructions, not only from Beth but from Dad too. Recently, so many of Beth's things had been broken by her younger siblings that Dad had declared Beth's room 'out of bounds'. But Beth could not go around threatening to cut off Gwenny's hair and get away with it.

Seconds later, Gwenny had picked up the glasses and decided to help herself to the manicure set too. Without the glasses and scissors Beth could not possibly cut off Gwenny's hair. She put them in her pocket and glanced towards the bed. The sleeping figure had not stirred but Gwenny froze as she saw the bedroom door swinging open. She was afraid; if it was Dad she would get an awful telling off. Gwenny's hands trembled and her body shivered. Her mouth felt dry as she bit her bottom lip. Then slowly, Muffin, the family cat, slunk into the room. He raised his tail when he saw Gwenny and he brushed past her bare legs with a tiny purr. Gwenny breathed a huge sigh of relief as Muffin crept under the bed.

With the glasses in her hand and the manicure set in her pocket, Gwenny went downstairs. But just as she reached the bottom step her foot slipped and she heard a dull thud as the glasses dropped out of her hand. She looked down in dismay as she saw Beth's glasses lying broken on the floor.

Oh no, thought Gwenny. She tried to piece together the bits but it was too late, the glasses were broken beyond repair. Her parents and Beth would never understand that she hadn't meant to break the glasses. They would never believe that she was only going to hide them for a little while. She opened the door to the hallway and tiptoed quickly down the passageway, past the parlour door and then into the scullery, where she could hear the sound of the wireless coming from the kitchen. As she closed the door from the hallway, she heard her Mum call out, 'Beth? Gwenny? Is that you?'

'If one of those girls is out of bed, I'll give them…' Dad started.

'Hush, Moc. There's no need to raise your voice. You'll wake the baby. I'm sure the girls are fast asleep, it's probably the cat.'

Gwenny froze and stood still. She did not want her parents to know that she was out of bed. So she hid behind the curtains and eavesdropped on their conversation.

'What are we going to do about Beth and Gwenny?' asked Mum.

'What do you mean?' replied Dad.

'They're quarrelling all the time and simply not being kind to each other.'

'They're only kids, haven't they always been like this?'

'I overheard Beth threatening to cut off Gwenny's plaits with a pair of scissors.'

'Well, hide the bloody scissors.'

'But, she wouldn't actually cut Gwenny's hair off. Would she?'

'Let's hope not. But haven't they argued since they were little? They're not a bit alike. Beth loves to get her own way, while Gwenny can be just as stubborn. That child goes around with her head in the clouds. She's always scribbling and making up little poems all day long. By the way, Clemmie doesn't help. Do you realise that he actually encourages her to write these poems?'

'Oh, you know she's his favourite. She's the spit of Annie with her blonde hair. To him she's the daughter they never had.'

'So what are we going to do?'

'I'll talk to Clemmie tonight.'

Gwenny didn't wait around for either of her parents to appear in the passage. She slipped her shoes and coat on and scurried down the garden path into the back lane. She had to find somewhere to hide. It was Sunday evening and even the church goers had long since returned to their homes. She walked to the end of the road where the ironmonger's shop stood on the street corner. She stopped by the back entrance of the shop and peered through the slats in the fence. The back yard would be a good place to hide. She tried the gate. It was open. She sneaked into the yard and shut the gate behind her. Then, Gwenny carefully picked her way across the flag-stoned yard. It was full of empty crates, cardboard boxes and tea chests all waiting to be disposed of when the rubbish was collected on Monday morning. Gwenny knew she had found the perfect place to hide for a couple of hours.

I'll creep into one of those boxes, she thought, *by the time they find me they won't be so angry that I broke Beth's glasses.*

Just then she heard the back door of the shop being unlocked so she quickly climbed into the nearest tea chest and pulled the flat cardboard boxes on top. She had only just covered her head when she heard men's voices.

'Easy man… easy', directed a man's voice.

'It's too heavy,' replied another voice.

'Where shall we put it man?'

'Over there… in the far corner.'

She listened as they lifted whatever they were carrying onto the chest she was in. Gwenny didn't move as she heard the footsteps move away and the back door being closed and locked. Then there was silence. The tea chest was full of soft paper packaging so Gwenny made herself as comfortable as possible. She began to imagine what was happening at home. By now, Mum would have gone to the bottom of the stairs to check on the children and found the broken glasses. Then she would have gone upstairs and discovered that Gwenny was missing. By now they would be searching the garden and questioning all the neighbours.

Mum will be here soon thought Gwenny as she moved her legs to a new position. It wouldn't be long now; Mum always found her when they played hide and seek.

'I'll just count to twenty,' Gwenny whispered to herself.

After that she chanted all the songs and rhymes that she had learnt with Clemmie. That kept her occupied for at least half hour then, she began to notice the silence again. One thought kept her going: that Mum would be here any minute, and with that she fell fast asleep.

Gwenny woke up confused and alarmed. Her arms and legs were stiff and she had no idea how long she had been asleep. Suddenly, she remembered where she was. She was still in the box and it was dark. She had better get home. She stretched out her arms above her head to remove the folded cardboard when she suddenly realised it would not move. Panicking she tried again. The cardboard box still would not shift and her common sense told her that someone, probably the men she had heard speaking, must have placed something heavy on top of the chest. What could she do? Would she ever get out? What if the rubbish men took her to the tip? The holes in the chest provided air gaps but she could not escape. Gwenny squeezed and pushed and thumped and bumped. She tried rocking from side to side, but the chest would not budge. Finally, in sheer desperation, she kicked the sides of the box but it was useless. She was stuck in the tea chest. If Beth hadn't threatened to cut off Gwenny's hair, she'd be safely tucked up in her bed. It was all Beth's fault.

'Mum, Mum,' she begun to cry, but her pleas went unheard. Her mum would be so worried; her dad would be so cross. She shuddered to think about how Beth would manage without her glasses. With these thoughts in mind, she cried herself into a very uncomfortable sleep.

She was woken by the sound of the rubbish van rumbling up the back lane. She could make out the men's voices as they called to each other. It was a familiar sound on a Monday morning. She could hear the back gate being opened. She called out, trying to make her voice heard, but she knew they could not hear her cries for help over the rumble of the lorry.

Then, she had an idea. She undid her plaits and quickly tied the two ribbons together. She was so glad that Clemmic had spent time showing her how to tie her shoelaces. She pushed the ribbon out through a tiny hole using the nail scissors, from Beth's manicure set, to push most of ribbon outside the chest. Then, very slowly, she pulled the long length of ribbon in and out of the hole, making sure that she didn't pull it too far. The distant noise from the van indicated to her that the bin men were moving on. Inside the yard there were no longer any voices. They hadn't heard her…she was going to have to stay in the box.

By now, panic and frustration had set in and she banged on the sides of the box with all her strength. Nearby, Dai Davies was just making a last visit to the yard to pick up the remains of the cardboard boxes. As he approached the corner of the yard, he thought he heard a thumping sound coming from one of the tea chests. He was about to turn away when he saw a bright pink ribbon poking out through one of the holes. The ribbon was moving and as he approached the tea chest; the sound of banging came louder and louder. Then, he heard a muffled voice calling, 'Help!'

'Hey, Gwyn, did you just hear that? Ask Mervyn to turn the engine off for a minute.'

The two men listened and then noticed that the pink ribbon was being pulled in and out of one of the little holes. They lifted the heavy iron unit off the top of the chest and peered inside. Gwenny cowered lower into the tea chest. She shielded her eyes from the unexpected bright sunlight.

'Hey girlie. What are you doing hiding in there?'

Gwenny blinked and stared up at the men. Her tangled, unplaited hair and tear stained face made it hard for anyone to recognise her. Then Dai spoke, his voice was kind and full of concern.

'You're Gwenny Evans, aren't you? The whole village has been up all night searching for you.'

cHAPTER tEN - 'yOU'RE gWENNY eVANS'

cHILDREN'S cANCER wARD, sOUTHAMPTON (1976)

'You're Gwenny Evans, aren't you?' said a voice through the intercom. Gwenny turned in surprise. It was James, the new boy in Day Ward. He was speaking to her.

'By the way, I'm James…James Harrington. I hope you don't mind but Jackie, the hospital teacher, told me your name. She said that you're the only other teenager on the ward right now so I thought I'd say hi…' he paused.

'No… no, I don't mind.' she smiled, swallowing hard and desperately trying to think what to say next. 'Jackie's a great teacher… isn't she?'

'So how come you get your own room and private facilities?'

'You've got to have a different sort of cancer,' she answered, feeling her cheeks go red and saying the first words that came into her head.

'So… Gwenny Evans, what sort of different cancer have you got then?' he asked, perching on the end of a chair, outside her window.

'Leukaemia. I had an operation a couple of weeks ago and I have to spend six weeks in isolation. What about you?'

'Well, it's a type of cancer, but they think it might be a type of leukaemia because of this massive bruise. He pushed up his sleeve and showed her his arm.

'Wow,' exclaimed Gwenny, 'that's quite a bruise!'

'Well, I'd better go and find my nurse now. Perhaps I'll see you again?'

'I'm won't be going anywhere,' stated Gwenny simply.

'You're not going back to Wales then?' he joked. It made her smile.

'Not now I've met you,' she whispered, as he turned and walked back to Day Ward.

James
Gwenny A. Harrington
James
LOVE LOVE LOVE
James Harrington
Gwenny Harrington
J.H
LOVES
G.A.E
forever
James and Gwenny
Gwenny
James
James
forever
Gwenny
Gwenny
Gwenny
James
James

Monday, February 9 (10.02 a.m.)

*My heart missed a beat a few minutes ago. In fact, I think I actually stopped breathing. My mind went completely blank as James Harrington, the boy I have fancied for ages, spoke to me for the very first time. I will write that again in capital letters. I SPOKE TO JAMES HARRINGTON TODAY. I still can't believe it! He's so good looking. He has the bluest eyes in the whole world. * N.B. I need to find out if he's got a girlfriend! I love everything about him. I absolutely love the way he says my name 'Gwenny Evans' in his lovely English accent. I am so excited. I am beside myself with joy. I cannot stop smiling. I don't know how to carry on. I haven't a clue what to write next. I am in a complete dither. I am doodling like mad. 'Gwenny. loves James.' in hearts with hearts and flowers and arrows and kisses. I've even started writing my new married name Gwendoline Ann Harrington; it has a certain ring to it. I have also begun practising my new signature ' G. A. Harrington' all over my exercise book. I'll have to tear out the pages in case someone sees. BUT I am over the moon. I am ecstatic. I suddenly feel like a brand new person. I can't wait to speak to him again. He is so gorgeous. I am actually glad I'm HERE...in hospital, or I would never have met him. I must write down the words for my next poem right now...*

To James, the new patient on the ward

I met you today

You have the most amazing eyes.

I spoke to you today

I will never forget your first words.

You smiled at me today.

I loved your cheeky grin and

The way you wrinkled up your nose.

The memory of your face will be etched on my heart forever;

The moment I fell in love for the very first time.

Tuesday, February 10 (8.30 a.m.)

Yesterday was one of the happiest days of my life but today is the saddest day ever. This morning as I sat on my bed hugging my mum, I watched in horror as the ward sister wiped little Ahmed's name off the large whiteboard outside my room. I was speechless as she erased all Ahmed's details and then left a very white blank space. I stared at that empty space for ages while I thought of the last time I'd seen Ahmed as he rode a small tricycle down the corridor. I pictured him as he ran away from his mum when she was trying to feed him. I remembered his big, beautiful smile and his dark brown eyes. I could not believe he had died in his sleep last night. My mum said one of the nurses had told her that Ahmed had caught an infection and his body couldn't fight it off. Everyone in the ward, even the doctors and nurses, are deeply affected. No one smiled this morning and the nurses came around and tactfully asked the parents to draw the curtains around their child's bed until the porters had wheeled Ahmed's body out.

My mum's here because it's half term, but we didn't say a word to each other as we listening to the trolley trundle past my room. I couldn't help noticing that all the televisions on the ward had been turned off. I spotted Ahmed's mum, through the gap in the curtains, she was supported by her family as they slowly walked behind the trolley. I felt so sorry for them. This is the first death I have witnessed since I came into hospital. I realise now that must happen all the time. It has made me think seriously about death. I must write down how I feel:-

To God

Why did you pick on me to have cancer?

Why when you were sorting out my life

Did you decide to say to me -

'Gwenny, you have to fight for your life.'

But God,

As I lie here in my bed,

What I really don't understand

Is...

Why did you let Ahmed, age five die?

What did he do to you?

What did he ever do wrong?

Why, God?

Why did you pick on him?

Just writing these words (it's not meant to be a poem) has helped me release some of my feelings about Ahmed's death. It simply isn't fair. BUT I am a fighter and I'm not staying in this place for one minute longer than I have to. I feel like a dried up old prune in here. I'm getting out of here as soon as I can.

I AM NOT LEAVING HERE IN A BOX!

12.00 noon - It's been really hard to do anything today because Ahmed has died. But as the morning wore on the ward gradually got back to normal. Jackie brought in the typewriter she had promised me so at last I am able to type up my poems.

<u>*Wednesday, February 11 (8.00 a.m.)*</u>

It's snowing. I can't believe my eyes. Why does all this whiteness make me feel so different? I feel so isolated, so cut off from the real world. In fact, I've never seen the car park so empty. I couldn't tear myself away from the window this morning as I watched people struggling to make their way to work on foot. I looked through Clemmie's binoculars and was utterly mesmerised as I watched the tiny flakes of snow cover absolutely everything. Even now I am amazed that anyone has managed to walk, let alone drive. Now I understand why my mum phoned me last night and explained that she wouldn't be coming to visit me this morning. Everything has been cancelled today unless it is an absolute emergency. The corridor is deserted and there are no parents rushing around. Everyone is waiting for the morning porters and I realise that I am actually <u>missing</u> the arrival of the breakfast trolley. Wednesday is clinic day which is usually a very busy day on the ward. There are always patients waiting for blood transfusions or operations, but today everything is eerily quiet. It's as if the snow has crept silently under the doors and into our ward. There are no visitors, no teachers, no therapists and only a handful of doctors and nurses.

Half an hour later, Gwenny watched, with great excitement, as a nurse printed the new patient's name on the whiteboard.

BED 10 - JAMES MICHAEL HARRINGTON - D.O.B - 04.09.61 - NURSE - KAY DUNKLEY

Ten minutes later.

'Hello again, Gwenny Evans,' greeted James.

'So you've finally been admitted to the ward then?'

'Yes, last night…before the heavy snowfall. Not even the snow could keep me away.'

'You won't be so cheerful once your chemo has started.'

'So what advice have you got for me?'

'Number one…use the mouthwash they prescribe you. The chemo, for some reason, makes your mouth really sore. Number two…don't eat the hospital meals when you're on chemo. Both together are guaranteed to make you throw up.'

'Everything?'

'Everything!'

'And what about the overnight chemo my nurse was just telling me about?'

'It's fine, if they manage to get the 'chemo up' before you go to sleep. If that happens, the sickness is much easier to cope with because you are asleep when the side effects hit you. Try and get your parents to insist you have overnight chemo… mine did.'

'Okay. I'll remember that. Thanks for the advice, *Auntie* Gwenny Evans.'

Then, with a cheeky grin, he span around and walked back to the four beds ward further along the corridor.

'I'll speak to you later,' Gwenny called after him, but he didn't turn around.

'How will he ever be my boyfriend if I can't get out of here?' she muttered crossly to herself.

Gwenny was still in a bad mood when Mum arrived that evening after the roads had been cleared of snow. She stamped her feet in the middle of the room and yelled at her mum in her loudest voice.

'I hate it here. And I'm not staying here a minute longer!'

Mum ducked as Gwenny's books and clothes were thrown across the room completely missing the bed and landing in a heap on the floor. Then, dragging her drugs trolley behind her, Gwenny barged into the bathroom gathering up her toiletries and stuffing them into her toilet bag. As she re-emerged from the bathroom, she shouted at her mum again, 'I am <u>not</u> having any more chemo. It makes me sick and I don't care if I'm neutropenic or not. I'm coming home. I've had enough.'

Gwenny was standing beside the bathroom door, looking a sorry sight. Her wig had slid to the side exposing 'wispy strands' of blonde hair.

'Mum, you're not listening to me.'

'I'm listening Gwenny,' said Mum glancing towards the doorway, realising that Clemmie had just arrived.

'I feel claustrophobic in here. I can't breathe properly. I can't be here anymore. Help me pack my bag Mum. I'm leaving now.'

Mum didn't move.

'I really mean it. Pleeeeease. Please Mum,' Gwenny pleaded looking at her mother in desperation. There was a short silence as Gwenny furiously rubbed her eyes.

'Mum, why aren't you packing?' Gwenny stuttered, as finally she broke down and the tears started running down her flushed cheeks.

Just at that moment Clemmie, gowned and masked, entered the room and Mum breathed a sigh of relief. He hugged Mum and indicated for her to leave. Then, he walked over to Gwenny.

'Gwenny,' he said turning her around to face him and removing his mask. 'You can't leave here. The doctors and nurses are doing everything they can to keep you alive. If we take you home now… you **will** die.'

Gwenny's body shuddered, still sobbing. Clemmie held her shoulders while she tried to regain her composure. She attempted to speak, but her body quivered with emotion.

'I... I don't... I don't... want to die,' she sniffed.

'So put your things back Gwenny. You **need** the treatment,' Clemmie said, slowly nodding his head. 'You **need** to stay in hospital.'

She looked up at Clemmie with reddened eyes, still trying to catch her breath after all the crying. He held her hand and spoke, 'Caraid...cariaid. Why did it have to be you? What have you ever done to deserve this?'

Then he took her in his arms, stroking her hair, as she whimpered his name. 'Clemmie, Clemmie.'

'Hush now Gwenny. We won't let you die. We realise how hard it is for you, but the treatment is going to make you well again. Only a few more weeks and we'll be taking you home.'

He paused, then he continued, 'Now go and get your lavender oil and I will massage you feet like I used to when you were small.'

'Oh Clemmie, I love you so much.'

'I know Gwenny.'

'Remember when I was little, I used to ask you how much you loved me. You used to stretch out your arms and you would say *I love you more than the highest mountain*.'

'Gwenny, I still love you more than the highest mountain.'

'Even when I chuck my things at Mum?'

'Well, I don't like your behaviour. That's why I came to help your Mum out. But I hope you know that I've always loved you since the moment I placed you in your mother's arms. Gwenny, you mean the world to me, you'll always be my special little girl born into my arms at Miskin House.'

cHAPTER eLEVEN - uP tHE mOUNTAIN

sEVEN sISTERS (1969)

It was poetry homework and all the children in Gwenny's class groaned loudly. Gwenny, on the other hand, was delighted. She wondered what all the fuss was about. She was so excited and she couldn't wait to tell Clemmie when they went for their walk up the mountain the next day.

Gwenny already knew what she was going to write her poem about it. It would be about her beloved valley. She enjoyed going for walks with Clemmie, who had lived in the valley all his life. Gwenny loved to hear about how the coal mining had first started and how all the men from neighbouring valleys had walked the mountains to find work at the new Seven Sisters Colliery. One of the young miners had been Gwenny's great grandfather. He had found lodgings in her great grandmother's house. There he had fallen in love and married her great grandmother. There were portraits of her great grandparents above the dresser in her auntie's living room. Gwenny always thought her great grandmother looked like a boy because all her hair was pinned back from her face. The other portrait was of her dark and distinguished-looking great grandfather. Gwenny felt very fortunate she that she had such good looking ancestors.

Clemmie, Beth and Gwenny had just reached the top of the mountain when Gwenny suddenly stopped walking and gazed back down on the valley.

'My stomach feels all wobbly.'

'I have those 'flutterflies' in my tummy.'

'Do you mean you have butterflies in your tummy?' asked Clemmie.

'Yes… it's the view from up here its soooooo beautiful.'

'That's the poet in you Gwenny, you feel things so intensely. You're so much like your grandmother. She was always saying how much she loved the valley. Why don't you write down how you feel? You could use the lines to write a poem for your homework.'

'But I haven't got any paper or a pencil.'

'I always carry a small pencil in my pocket and you can use the back of my *Woodbine* packet. Go on Gwenny…give it a go.'

'Okay, I will. I'll write down the words as they come into my head.'

'Why don't you sit on that boulder over there and I'll call Beth. Your sister and I need to have a little chat while you are writing.'

He walked quickly to the end of the track and called to Beth, who had walked ahead, 'Beth, we're going to take a five minute break here. Gwenny needs to write her poem for school.'

'Why do we always have to stop when she wants to?' complained Beth, trudging back up the slope.

'Hey, Beth that's not fair. You chose the spot where we stopped for our picnic. It's Gwenny's turn now.'

'But I didn't have to write a soppy poem. I did my homework after school like you're supposed to do. Gwenny should have done hers then.'

'I couldn't think of anything to write about,' Gwenny chipped in.

'That's because you always make a fuss about everything.'

'No, I don't.'

'Oh yes, you do. You always run to Mum when you can't get your own way.'

'That's enough, you two,' interrupted Clemmie.

Gwenny and Beth stopped.

'Now you go over there and write your poem. Beth, I want to have a word with you.'

Clemmie put his jacket down on the grass. Beth came and sat by his side.

'Beth, I don't want you quarrelling with Gwenny all the time. Your mum has heard you saying some very nasty things to Gwenny.'

'No, I haven't,' protested Beth.

'Oh, yes you have. You threatened to cut off her plaits while she was asleep and as a result Gwenny broke your glasses. And I know she was wrong for taking your glasses but do you realise that we all nearly went out of our minds with worry when she went missing.'

'Well, I really don't like Gwenny right now, and I really **hate** her hair.'

'That's no way to speak about your little sister.'

'She only ran away because she wanted to get attention. She always gets Mum's attention.'

'That's not true. Your mum tries to give each one of you her individual attention. She took you out on your own, in the school holidays, to get a new school uniform for grammar school.'

'Yes I know, but Gwenny always has Mum's attention when I would like Mum to myself...like when she can't get to sleep. Mum goes into her room and reads her a story.'

'I remember your mum always reading you stories when you were Gwenny's age. Now you're a little older and she knows you can read your own stories.'

'I wish I wasn't the oldest.'

'Well, you had your mum all to yourself for four years before Gwenny was born but I will remind her that you still need time on your own with her. I'm sure she will do her best…like she always does.'

'I'm fed up now,' moaned Beth, 'we've sat here for ages.'

'Be patient, Beth. Gwenny won't be much longer.'

A few minutes later, Gwenny finished writing. She came running over to join Clemmie and Beth.

'Clemmie, I've finished. Do you want to hear?'

She read the lines out loud:

I love my valley
When I go for a walk up the mountain
I am so happy.
I feel as if I am on the top of the world.
I can see all the things that are important in my life.
I can see my house
I can see Clemmie's cottage
I can see my school and Dad's colliery.
I can see the church where we go on Sundays.
I can see the river we paddle in.
I love the way it glistens in the sun.
My valley is very special to me.
It is my home.
It is where my family come from.
It is where I belong.

'Well done Gwenny,' exclaimed Clemmie. 'You just need to polish it up a bit and you'll be able to enter it into the poetry competition at the Eisteddfod.'

They arrived home exhausted after their long walk up the mountain. Gwenny's fair skin was bright pink where she had caught the sun. Mum suggested having a wash in the washstand in her parent's bedroom. Gwenny felt refreshed after her wash, but Mum insisted on plastering her face and arms in calamine lotion. Gwenny didn't like the smell it made her sneeze.

'Atishoo, atishoo,' sneezed Gwenny.

'Bless you love.'

Mum hugged her, 'Gwenny, don't you ever run away again. We were so worried. But listen you're a big girl now so you will have to finish getting ready for bed by yourself,' said Mum. 'The little ones are downstairs with Clemmie and I need to get their supper before they go to sleep.'

'Okay, Mum, I can manage now.'

Mum went downstairs and Gwenny put on her summer nightie, which was really her winter nightie with the sleeves cut off. But Gwenny didn't notice her makeshift nightie, she was too busy thinking of how she could improve the poem she had started that afternoon. She needed to put in some adjectives. Her teacher always said that if you put in some good describing words, the reader could conjure up pictures. Gwenny gathered up the clothes she had left on the bedroom floor and carried them out onto the landing where she placed them in the large Ali Baba linen basket. She was still reciting the poem to herself when she became aware that the door of her bedroom was opening slowly. Beth crept out.

Gwenny startled Beth when she called out, 'What were you doing in my room?'

'Oh Gwenny you gave me such a fright! I nearly jumped out of my skin. You look like a ghost with that calamine lotion on your face.' Beth smothered a giggle.

'Look, I was only borrowing your little dictionary.'

She held up the small leather book in her hand.

'Well, you could have asked.' replied Gwenny.

'I couldn't because you were having a wash. I didn't think you would mind.'

'You wouldn't like it if I went into your bedroom without asking you first.'

Beth shrugged her shoulders.

'Here… have your old dictionary,' she said, shoving the book into Gwenny's chest. 'It's not even yours. It's Mum's old one from when she was a child.'

Gwenny returned to the bedroom she shared with Rosie. Everything seemed to be in place, but she was still puzzled why Beth had been in her room borrowing her dictionary. Beth had already finished her homework, she had said so earlier on. Also, Gwenny was sure that Dad had bought Beth a pocket dictionary for her birthday.

A short while later Clemmie came upstairs to say goodnight to Gwenny. She was sitting on her bed with the contents of her kit bag all over the eiderdown.

'The cigarette packet I wrote my poem on; it's not in my bag.'

'It must be there,' said Clemmie. 'Here, let me look. I put it in the front pocket,'

'Well, it's gone. It must have fallen out on the way home.'

'Oh dear, now you won't be able to write your poem.'

'I'll just have to start again.'

'Can you remember it?'

'Well, I remember some words but it won't be exactly the same.'

'Okay, do your best. I'm just going to say goodnight to Beth.'

Beth had been listening to the conversation outside Gwenny's door and she moved quickly to get back to her bedroom before she was caught eavesdropping. In her hand she held a crumpled piece of card. It was pale and green. On the side of the card was one word *'Woodbine'*.

cHAPTER tWELVE – bEAUTY qUEEN

cHILDREN'S cANCER wARD, sOUTHAMPTON (1976)

'James, have you or anyone in your family ever smoked?' asked Gwenny, picking up the letter from the 'Cancer UK Research Study.'

'No, why do you ask?'

'I was just wondering. This survey is asking a lot of questions about smoking. I suppose they think it might be one of the reasons we have cancer.'

'Why? Have you ever smoked then, Gwenny Evans?'

'No way, not with a father like mine. But I did spend a lot of time, when I was younger, with my uncle, who was always smoking *Woodbine* cigarettes. Do you remember I mentioned my Uncle Clemmie to you?'

'Yes I **do** remember, Gwenny Evans.'

'Why don't you call me Gwenny like everyone else does?' she said, putting down the survey.

'Because I'm not everyone else, and I love the sound of your name. It has a certain ring to it. You couldn't come from anywhere else but Wales with a name like Gwenny Evans.'

'But nobody calls me Gwenny Evans.'

'Well I do, so there.'

She wrinkled her nose and smiled.

'So when's your chemo starting?'

'They haven't even mentioned it yet because the consultant is snowed in.'

'Like everyone else,' they both said together. They burst out laughing.

'I can't get over that. We said those words at exactly the same time. Can you read my mind?'

'I wish I could. I'm beginning to feel like a spare part around here.'

'Yeah, it's not a good start. They can't give you chemo and they can't send you home because of the snow.'

'I'm here just to enjoy the view.'

'I thought you said you had a room around the back.'

'Yes, it overlooks the hospital kitchens. Some view! I don't get my own room like you… little girlie.'

'Me? Girlie? I don't even look like a girl any more.'

'But you are such a girlie with your pink dressing gown, your big fluffy slippers, your pierced earrings and pink nail varnish. You may have no hair at the moment, but you're definitely a girl who loves girlie things.'

'Umm…I suppose I am.'

'By the way, you're the winner of my competition.'

'What competition? I can't remember entering one?'

'I made it up the other day when I was trying to decide who was the prettiest girl on the ward… you won the first prize!'

Then, he produced a piece of cardboard attached to a long string. It said *First Prize Awarded to Gwenny Evans, Beauty Queen of Pearl Ward 1976.*

'You were voted the winner unanimously.'

'Who were the judges?'

'Let me think… there was me, me and me.'

She grinned.

'What's the first prize?'

'You get a very special handmade crown.'

He took it out of a paper bag.

'Thanks, but I can't actually have it in my room.

'Oops, sorry, I forgot. But don't worry. I'll place it by your window with your cardboard necklace.'

She laughed as he attempted to prop the homemade items on the windowsill. They instantly fell off. Gwenny giggled.

'Thank you James. I don't feel much like a beauty queen right now but you do make me laugh!

<u>*Thursday, February 12 (11.00 a.m.)*</u>

I haven't smiled or laughed so much since I came into hospital. James is such a joker and a lovely friend to have around. But we'll never be a proper boyfriend and girlfriend because there is always a glass panel between us. We can't even have a private conversation because there is always someone, who can overhear what we are saying to each other. I must tell James how I feel.

One hour later.

'I just want to hear your voice actually speaking to me,' Gwenny moaned to James.

'Gwenny Evans,' he exasperated. 'Even if I gave you the moon and stars that wouldn't be enough for you but… I'll see what I can do.'

He peered through the window staring at the phone that was on the bedside table.

'Just wait a moment. I've got an idea.'

He returned in a few minutes wheeling the phone trolley and plugging it into the nearest phone socket. Then, he got a ten pence coin out of his pocket and dialled the number. Gwenny tapped the window.

'James…James…who are you phoning?'

At that exact moment, the phone in Gwenny's room rang and she picked up the receiver. The pips sounded telling her that the person on the other end of the line needed to put coins in. She watched through her window as James placed the coins in the slot.

'Hello…Gwenny Evans,' greeted the voice on the other end of the phone. He grinned at her through the glass.

'Who's speaking please?' she questioned, pretending she didn't know.

Then she laughed, 'James, stop mucking around.'

'It's your knight in shining armour and I love the sound of your voice. It's your welsh accent, it's even more pronounced on the phone. I love it!'

'Really?'

'Really. You are officially my beauty queen.'

'And you're my knight in shining armour.'

Their eyes met through the glass.

'We can talk privately at last. No one else can hear us.'

'James, this is great. But I've been meaning to ask you something for ages. Have you got a girlfriend?'

'No… but it's not any of your business… little Miss Nosey Parker.'

'Why not?'

'Because all the girls that go to my school are stuck up bitches,' he answered, lowering his voice. 'They all come from families who have pots of money. I had to pass a scholarship to get into my school. I won't tell you what they call me, but it's not a very nice name.'

'Well, you're better off out of a school like that. It may be a private school but the kids there sound exactly like the ones at my school. I get called unkind names because of my accent.'

'Gwenny Evans, promise me you'll never ever change your accent. It makes you the unique person you are today. Why have you never come into my life before?'

'Because it's in our stars… we were destined to meet here.'

'Do you actually believe that?'

'I do!'

The pips beeped and the line went dead.

'I love you James,' she thought, *'love you, love you, love you.'*

She watched him unplug the phone trolley and wheel it back up the corridor.

'James Harrington. I am head over heels in love with you.' she repeated to herself over and over again.

Thursday, February 12 (2.00 p.m.)

It's still snowing. I keep looking out of the window and seeing a completely new world. The car park is treacherous today and there are hardly any vehicles. The world's so silent without cars and buses. I can't even remember hearing an aeroplane fly past in the last couple of hours. The doctors and nurses are rushed of their feet because so many parents haven't been able to visit. I was lucky that my mum managed to visit last night before the heavy snowfall. James has been only been down the corridor once today. Perhaps he isn't feeling too good. Oh God... why is time moving so slowly? And why do I have to wear these silly glasses? They keep slipping off my nose!

Minutes later. James walked past the window

'Hey girlie, have you got a cob on?'

'No, I'm not in a bad mood. I'm sad because my mum can't get here today.'

'I've just had a good idea…let's make up a secret code. Then, we won't have to speak in front of other people, we'll just give each other signals. For example, if you need to speak to me, leave a white tissue on the window sill. Then I'll know that you want me to stop and have a chat.'

'But how will I know that you want to speak to me?'

'I'll do the same. I will leave a tissue sticking out of my pocket so when you see it, you will know that I want to speak to you.'

'We're going to need a lot of tissues.'

'Well… when I walk past at the moment, I never know if you want to talk or not. Sometimes you may be tired and you don't know how to tell me without offending me.'

'I suppose you could always write me a note.'

'Yes I could. But someone else would have to disinfect it first.'

'We will need some signal that means stop too.'

'That will have to be a hand signal,' he said, putting his hand up to demonstrate. 'Like this…let's try it out.'

'James?'

'What?'

'It's just a hand signal. Don't treat at me as if I'm complete moron.'

'I'm not. I was just thinking your wig is all wonky. Have you got it on the right way round?' he continued, signalling for her to stop talking.

'Oh no,' exclaimed Gwenny, appalled. 'Have I got it on back to front? I've worn it like this all morning and you haven't even mentioned it.'

She got up from her chair and went to the mirror. James was trying out the stop signal, but Gwenny wasn't taking any notice.

'Hey,' he said pausing and waiting for her to focus her attention, 'I was only teasing; your wig is fine. I was just trying out our new stop signal, which obviously doesn't work because you weren't taking any notice. Gwenny Evans you're such a little kid. When are you ever going to grow up?'

cHAPTER tHIRTEEN – eISTEDDFOD

mINER'S hALL, sEVEN sISTERS (1971)

Gwenny ran all the way to school. She had butterflies in her tummy because she had made her very first grown up decision. She had decided that she was going to enter a poem in the poetry competition at the local eisteddfod. She had worked very hard on her poem about her valley. When it was ready she wrote it out in her neatest handwriting and was just about to post it in the competition box when her younger sister, Rosie, came running down the corridor. Gwenny quickly stuffed the envelope back into her satchel.

'What are you doing Gwenny?' asked Rosie.

'Oh, I was just going to check with Miss Williams if I could take the registers,' answered Gwenny, saying the first thing that came into her head.

She waited for Rosie to make her way to her classroom and then she removed the envelope from her satchel. She looked at the title *My Valley* by Tiger Lily. She couldn't quite remember where she had got that pen name from. It was probably from some book she had read. Inside an attached sealed envelope was her real name.

Her hands trembled as she put the envelope in the box. Her stomach churned as she realised that it was the first time in her life that she had made an important decision without consulting her parents. But it would be worth it. She couldn't wait to see her father's face when she won the prize. He would be so proud of her. She would show her dad that she wasn't stupid.

The Eisteddfod day arrived at last. Gwenny's school assembled with the senior school at the Miner's Hall. The room was light and airy, there was a wide curtained stage and very high ceilings. The whole room buzzed with children's voices as the adults tried to quieten their students. As her class were shown to their seats, Gwenny turned to the girl in front of her and said, 'Excuse me, do you mind if I change places with you? I'd like to sit in an aisle seat so I can see my sister.'

Gwenny had already spotted Beth sitting with the older children several rows behind. Gwenny wanted to make sure that Beth would see her when she went up to receive her prize. Gwenny's excitement mounted as the head teacher of her school climbed the steps to the stage. Miss Williams paused a moment and waited for silence. Then, she picked up the microphone and spoke in a clear voice,

'I would like to welcome you all to our annual Eisteddfod. Thank you to all the teachers who have brought their classes here today. Also, I'd like to thank all the pupils who have entered our choral speaking and poetry competitions. We'll start the afternoon with the choral speaking groups. Then, after the break, I'll announce the winners of the poetry competition.'

The choral groups were very well-rehearsed, but they went on and on. Gwenny was so bored she just couldn't keep still. She wriggled on her chair and moved her legs so many times that the teacher, who was sitting behind her hissed in her ear.

'Keep still Gwenny. What's the matter with you today?'

But at last, the moment she had been waiting for arrived. Gwenny perched on the very end of her seat as the head teacher began to announce the winners. In reverse order, Miss Williams called out the names of the third and second prizes. Gwenny listened carefully *Good* she thought to herself. *My name hasn't been called out yet so I must have won the first prize*. First prize - what an honour! She had never been won anything in her life. Gwenny relished the chance to shine at something. Suddenly, the clear tones of the head's announcement interrupted her dreams. She waited with her fingers crossed and hardly daring to breathe.

'I have great pleasure in awarding the first prize to,' Miss Williams paused as she broke the seal on the envelope, 'Gwendoline Evans.'

Gwenny didn't wait to hear any more. She was so elated that she shot out of her seat. Her feet didn't touch the ground as she made her way up to the stage to collect the first prize. As she walked towards the stage Gwenny's shoulders were tall and upright and she smiled broadly at the other children. She was so overwhelmed that she completely shut out her surroundings. She couldn't wait to tell her father that she was good at something. She imagined his face. He would congratulate her and hug her tightly. In her daze, she was aware of many voices and she guessed that they were cheering her. She was also aware of hands pointing to someone, but her only thought was about what her father would say when he saw the trophy.

But Gwenny's moment of triumph was to be very short lived. Her heart sank as moments later the head teacher, who towered above her, bent down and spoke gently, almost in a whisper.

'Gwenny dear, it's Gwendoline Evans from the senior school, who has won the first prize.'

Gwenny turned around as an older girl, with a winning smile, climbed the steps to the stage.

Gwenny was mortified. She turned around and crept back to her seat with her shoulders bent. She did not dare make eye contact with anyone. Her cheeks were flushed with embarrassment. She wished that the ground would swallow her up. She tried to ignore the stares, but she heard the smothered giggles and heard the taunts.

Gwenny didn't look but she heard one girl saying…

'She's so stupid. She can't even write a poem.'

Gwenny didn't remember leaving the Miner's Hall that day. She decided to walk home alone rather than catch the school bus. She arrived home to hear Beth's voice in the kitchen.

'She was so stupid that she thought she'd won the first prize. She even went up on the stage. What a complete idiot she made of herself. I was so embarrassed. I didn't tell anyone that she was my sister.'

'Listen Beth,' answered Mum, 'I've heard quite enough from you. Never mind about your embarrassment. Just imagine how Gwenny must be feeling right now. She hasn't even come home on the school bus. So…no more of your gloating. At least Gwenny tried; you didn't even enter the competition.'

'But I'm no good at poetry.'

'I know but Gwenny is. She loves her writing and, unfortunately, on this occasion it wasn't good enough. But Gwenny has learnt an important lesson today: how to cope with disappointment. The last thing she needs is you going on about it. Now, be a good girl and keep an eye on the little ones. I'm just going to look up the road to check if she's on her way home.'

Mum walked across the scullery and opened the back door. She stopped suddenly as she almost tripped over Gwenny, who was sitting on the back doorstep. Her eyes were red from crying, 'Oh, Mum,' she sniffed. 'I wanted you and Dad to be proud of me.'

Mum sat down next to Gwenny, pulled her in close and hugged her, 'We are proud of you Gwenny.'

'But I didn't win.'

'But you tried. You did your best and that's all we ever want you to do. I think you did a really brave thing. Well done for having a go.'

'Will you tell Dad?'

'Yes, we'll have to because if we don't tell him someone else will. It'll be better coming from us.'

Gwenny smiled through her tears.

'Now, wipe your eyes,' consoled Mum, taking a hankie out of her apron pocket. 'Hang your coat up; we've got to boil the eggs for tea.'

cHAPTER fOURTEEN - gOING hOME

cHILDREN'S cANCER wARD, sOUTHAMPTON (1976)

Gwenny and James were having one of their daily conversations through the window of her isolation ward.

'James, what do you miss most when you're in hospital?' asked Gwenny.

'I miss tons of things. But right now, right this minute, I really miss my mum's scrambled eggs!' answered James.

'Eggs? Ugh! I'm being serious James.'

'I am too. My mum's eggs are seriously good, I'll have you know. But, if you must have an answer, the thing I really miss is my own bedroom.'

'Oh, really? I didn't think you would say that.'

'What did you think I would say?'

'I thought you would say sailing because I know how much you love the sea. What about your mates that you go sailing with?'

'Yeah… I miss the whole crew. But when you get better…I'm going to take you sailing with us. You'll love sailing.'

Gwenny's face lit up. She had always loved the sea.

'Where will we go?'

'We'll go to Isle of Wight. Or maybe France. We might even go around the world.'

'And what will you do when my wig blows off?

'You'll have all your hair back by then.'

Gwenny shrugged her shoulders and quickly adjusted her wig, 'Do you know what I like about you James? You are the only one who says ***when*** *you get better.*

Everyone else avoids talking about the future…in case I'm not here!'

'Don't be daft… of course you're going to be here.'

'When… you just said '*We're going to sail around the world'* …I suddenly felt that my life's worth living again.'

Her face lit up as she spoke. There was a slight pause in their conversation.

'Gwenny Evans… I would love to hold your hand and touch your skin.'

'Right…do it then. Come through the door and just hold my hand. I dare you to, but I bet you haven't got the guts to do it, or have you?'

'Guts? I'll show you,' exploded James, strutting to the doorway that led into Gwenny's isolation room. He was just about to open the door when a nurse called out.

'James Harrington! What do you think you're doing?'

'Oh heck,' muttered James, as he instantly let go of the door handle and scampered away up the corridor.

Monday, February 16 (11.00 a.m.)

We had a right old telling off today from the ward sister. James was about to open my door for a dare. I don't think he would have actually come into my room, but he was really gutted at being caught so he hid down the corridor and phoned me instead. He put fifty pence in the box and we talked for ages. He says the nuttiest things…he called me a trouble maker! He said that I want the earth and he said that when I'm out of isolation he's going to take me up on the roof and show me the moon and stars. He says that he's even going to catch me a shooting star. I know he's talking complete and utter rubbish. But it's such a lovely thought. Seriously though, I keep imagining what it will be like when he kisses me. What will I do? Will my tongue get in the way? Will I make a complete and utter mess of it all? He won't want a girlfriend who cannot kiss. I'll have to practise my kissing in the bathroom with the door locked. I don't want anyone to see me practising my perfect kiss on the mirror. James does make me laugh though, especially when he insists on calling me Gwenny Evans...all of the time. But he's also got a serious side to his character. He's such a good listener. I don't know why but I decided to share with James the lines that I wrote in the middle of the night. I'm going to use them for one of my next poems.

Dark and menacing,

Invasive and personal,

It seeps through my body

It flows through my blood.

It drags me down with massive bruising,

It tires me out with a never ending weariness.

And

If that isn't enough to bear,

There is the chemotherapy

With the strange and complicated side effects,

The drugs make my veins feel cold and unfamiliar.

I am wired up to countless blood transfusions.

I am continually connected to bags of saline.

But

I will get better,

Because

I know in the end that I am going to beat this cancer,

I know that I am going to be the winner!

Tuesday, February 17 (11.00 a.m.)

Mum came earlier today. She was full of family gossip. Beth has a new boyfriend at university. She met him in her history lecture! Now I'll have to put up with a sister, who talks about the world wars! Boring!

Rosie has a place in the netball team. She's going to be an excellent player but I hope she'll practice at school because it really gets on my nerves when she practices her catches at home!

Gareth has got through the football trials and is now in the local school boys' football team. Dad must be pleased that he has a son to follow in his footsteps at last. I have such a lot to tell James.

James appeared outside Gwenny's room much later than usual the next day. Gwenny had just finished writing her journal and was replacing the tiny key on her silver chain.

'My mum called in on her way to work this morning,' Gwenny explained, 'I've loads of family gossip to share with you.'

She was just about to begin to tell James all her news when she stopped and looked at him. She noted how his shoulders were hunched and he wasn't making eye contact. He looked as if he had a lot on his mind.

'What's wrong James?' asked Gwenny. 'You haven't been listening to me prattling on. I can see your thoughts are elsewhere.'

'I don't want my mother finding out about us.' he started

'But…why not? I bet the nurses have already told her.'

'She doesn't have to know.'

'Why? Won't she approve?'

'I don't know. I've never had a girlfriend before and she has always told me that if I've got a girlfriend I won't pass my exams and if I don't get good grades I won't be able to go to university! She knows I've set my heart on going to Sheffield University.'

'But that's ridiculous James, I've told my mum all about you and she doesn't mind.'

James looked away and Gwenny sensed there was still something else.

'But James…you're all twitchy, that's not all is it?'

He turned and looked at her. She could tell he was nervous by the way he clenched his fists.

'Gwenny, I have something I need to say and I don't know how you'll react.'

'What? What is it James? Is it really bad news?'

'I'm going home today,' he blurted out.

'Home...HOME?' she choked. 'You can't go home yet. You still need your chemo.'

'No Gwenny. My treatment is a lot different from yours. Remember you predicted that I would loose my hair but I haven't. Also, I know you spent a long time in hospital having tests before your treatment started, but my protocol is different. I will need lots of short bursts of chemo and then I'll return to the ward as a day patient. My first course of chemo has finished and I'll be back in two weeks.'

Her face crumpled; there were tears in her eyes.

'But it won't be the same,' moaned Gwenny.

'I know that's why I made you this. It's something for you to look at after I've left.'

He held up an envelope. It had *Gwenny Evans* written on it in big scrawling letters.

'Thank you,' she said, turning to look the other way.

'I will leave it by the hatch so the nurses can spray the envelope. You'll have to wear your gloves when you open it.'

'But James,' she murmured, turning back to face him, 'I can't stay here without you.'

'Gwenny, don't be silly. You were here before we even met each other. You coped with the isolation ward then. Remember all the conversations we've had recently? I'm going to remind you what we agreed. You can do anything you want to do even if you have cancer'

'Not on my own. I c…c…can't. I can't stay here without you.'

'You only have to put up with it for a couple more weeks. Then… you'll be out of isolation.'

'But I won't be out of hospital. I will still have to stay for my treatment.'

'Yeah, but you'll be able to do lots more things; go to schoolroom, mix with the other kids again. It's just that you've been in there too long on your own. You've got all down in the dumps.'

'Oh, thank you for your diagnosis, Doctor Harrington. How come you know everything?'

'Because I'm really, really clever,' he shouted, suddenly changing the mood. 'I wasn't the one who had to go in the DUNCE'S class!'

He laughed as he ran off down the corridor.

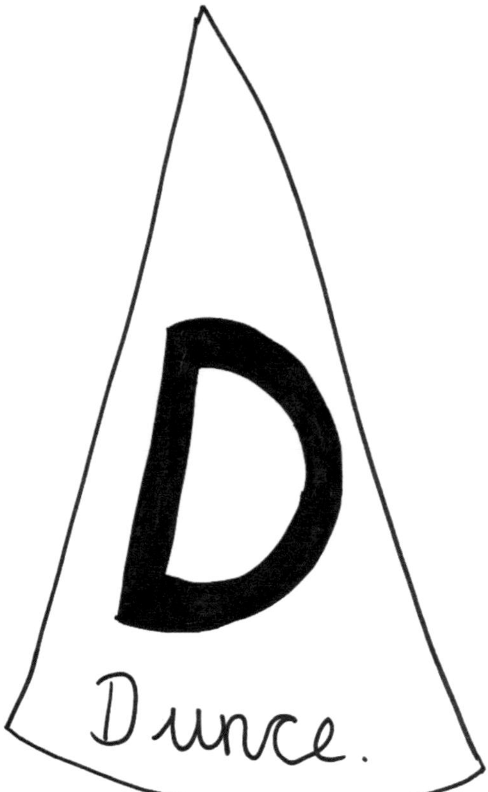
D
Dunce.

cHAPTER fIFTEEN - dEN oF dUNCES

sEVEN sISTERS (1971)

Gwenny and Clemmie were curled up together on the sofa. It was early evening and Gwenny's parents were having a rare evening out. Beth was upstairs doing her homework and the younger ones were in bed. For once, Gwenny had Clemmie all to herself.

'Clemmie,' she said, 'would you still love me if I was in the Dunces' class?'

'Oh, Gwenny, you don't half say some funny things? What made you ask that now?'

'Because everyone says I'm a dunce. Beth calls me a dunce and now all my school friends are calling me *Gwenny, the Dunce* because I didn't win the poetry competition last term. They even made me a dunces' hat out of paper.'

'Listen Gwenny. You are not a dunce. Beth and your school friends were very mean to call you that.'

'But Dad thinks I'm a dunce too. He took me to Archie's house so I could have arithmetic coaching for the eleven plus because he's worried that I won't pass.'

'Hang on a minute, little lady, of course you're going to pass. Dad was just trying to help you. You said yourself you're not so good at sums. To pass the eleven plus you have to pass all three papers; the English, the Verbal Reasoning and the Arithmetic.'

'I know that Clemmie, but it was awfully embarrassing going to Archie's house for coaching. I had to take my shoes off by the front door because his wife had just bought a new carpet. Then I had to sit in the front room with four boys. I didn't even know them!'

Gwenny wrinkled her nose in disgust.

'And… if that wasn't bad enough…because I was last one to arrive, I had to sit on the settee, right in the middle of two very smelly boys.'

'Gwenny. That's not a nice way for a young lady to talk. Why do you call them smelly?'

'Seriously Clemmie…they actually DID smell. They stunk of plasticine, plimsolls and sour milk. And… there were grass stains and mud all over their legs.'

'They'd probably gone there straight from school,' explained Clemmie. 'You were the lucky that you had time to go home to change your clothes.'

'Ah, but the smell was awful. Can I tell you what they were really doing?' Gwenny crept nearer whispered in Clemmie's ear. 'They were doing that word that Dad doesn't allow us to say. I'll spell it for you…f…a…r…t…s; really smelly ones. And worse than that, they were copying the answers out of the teacher's book every time Archie left the room. But they wouldn't give me the answers.'

'So why didn't you tell Archie?' asked Clemmie.

'I did say that I'd tell Archie…but they said that if I told on them, they would complain that I was making the stinky smells.'

'Oh, Gwenny, how many times did you go to Archie's house?'

'Three times I think.'

'Did you learn anything at all?'

'I learnt my times tables. I know them off by heart.'

'That's good. We all need our times tables.'

'Yeah, but I don't know how to use them when I'm doing my sums. Oh, I hate sums!' she clasped her fists together and started to cry.

'Gwenny,… Gwenny …stop that silliness right now. You may not be good at sums, but you are good at writing and you will pass the eleven plus. You're a good little scholar. Okay, I know you didn't win the poetry competition, but the winner was a lot older than you and she probably had some help from her teacher. You wrote your poem all by yourself and you even had a special mention in the school magazine for being the youngest child to enter. You will pass the eleven plus because I say you will.'

'Really, will I?'

'You will my darling.'

'Do you know anyone who failed?'

'Yes, but they were proper dunces...you're not a dunce. Now let's think what can we do?'

Clemmie drew her close to him and looked straight into her eyes.

'First of all I'll teach you everything I know about sums. Then, if you work hard and pass the exam, I promise I'll give you over five pounds to spend. Do you remember that long cardboard tube I had for Beth when she passed the eleven plus? Well, since she started grammar school I have been saving my coins in that tube for you. So when you pass the eleven plus Gwenny, there'll be lots of coins for you.'

'Oh Clemmie, thank you,' said Gwenny, giving him a big hug, 'I'll have more money than anyone in the whole world.'

'And you can spend it on anything you like.'

'Will I have enough for new books and a new ink pen?' asked Gwenny, her face lighting up.

'As many books and as many pens as you want to buy. But tell me, why didn't you carry on going to Archie's house? What happened to make you stop going there?'

'Well I was a little bit naughty.'

'Gwenny,' said Clemmie with a frown. 'What did you do?'

'Well, I couldn't do any of the mental arithmetic so I opened the teacher's book when Archie was out and copied all the correct answers into my book. Then, I purposely read out all the wrong answers to the boys. I wanted to get them back for the time when they wouldn't tell me any of the answers. But when Archie came back in the room I lost my courage and I began to worry about how they would react, so I decided that I had to get out of there pretty quick. In fact, I got so worried that when Archie came back into the room I made myself sick and I threw up all over Archie and the new carpet.' Gwenny stopped to take a breath, then, she continued. 'After that Archie told Dad that there was nothing more he could teach me. I think it had a lot to do with the carpet. What do you think Clemmie?'

cHAPTER sIXTEEN - bEING sICK tOGETHER

cHILDREN'S cANCER wARD, sOUTHAMPTON (1976)

Tuesday, 17 February (8.00 p.m.)

I have made a new word for the English Dictionary. The word is 'Jamesless'. I can't believe James has gone home and left me. I am now suffering from the sickness called 'Jamesless' and there is no cure, the only way I can recover is to see him again. I love him so much and I know deep down that he loves me too. It says so in his letter. In honour of his leaving I am going to make some plans. Plan A is to get on with my book and to write as many poems as I can in the time I have left in isolation. Plan B - there isn't one yet! So I'd better start the poems:-

Lonely,

Sad,

No one to talk to,

Empty,

Unmotivated,

Unhappy,

Left behind,

Stuck,

Emotional,

I am a nothing

I am 'Jamesless'.

'You throwing up again?' asked a familiar voice in a sympathetic tone. Gwenny was lying on her bed with her back to the window. She turned around and gasped as she saw James standing in the corridor staring into her room through the glass panel.

He was wearing a stack of sick bowls on his head.

'James! What are you doing here?' she gulped, 'I thought you'd gone home.'

'I've been home but I had to come back.'

'Oh, it's so good to see you, but why have you come back? Are you sick?'

'I've been feeling sick most of the time,' he answered. 'That's why I've been fetching more sick bowls.'

'Maybe you've got a stomach bug?'

'Oh, don't tell me it's only a stomach bug and I've come all the way back here.'

'Have you got a temperature?'

'Yeah, I've got one of those.'

Just then Gwenny bowed her head and retching, she moved the sick bowl closer to her mouth. She coughed a little spit into the bowl and looked up. 'Don't just stand there watching me throw up.'

'Your face is a picture, you look like a ghost.'

'You can talk. Have you looked in the mirror?'

'I'll go then, I can see you want to be left alone.'

'No, I'm okay for a minute.'

'I just wanted to be the one to tell you that I'm back.'

'Have you got a bed?'

'No, I'm in day ward until they find me one. You go back to your sick bowl.'

Just then he grabbed his bowl to his mouth and spluttered, 'Oops, got to go.'

back.'

'Oh, James,' she called after him, 'I forgot to say, I'm SO glad you're back.' He gave her a thumbs up sign as she watched him dash into the nearest toilet, clutching a bowl to his mouth.

Wednesday, 18 February (11.00 a.m.)

I've been feeling really sick all last night. The anti-sickness drug was playing me up again. It was strange that when I was feeling so lousy James turned up out of the blue…he made me feel so much better again so I instantly wrote these lines:-

My heart is smiling… I wonder if you can tell.
I just feel so full of joy that I am almost bursting at the seams.
I am like an explosion ready to erupt with millions and zillions of happy thoughts,
They are all stored up inside my head,
They are ready to explode like fizzling fireworks,
James is back!

'Only just made it in time,' he said, as he pulled up a chair to her window sometime later. He stacked the sick bowls on a nearby table.

'You can spare me the details. I really think you should be in bed.'

'I'm fine now but I was feeling really bad when I got home so my mum phoned the ward manager's office. They said that if I had a temperature, I was to come straight back here at once.'

'You didn't have much time at home then.'

'No, just long enough to feed the cats. When my mum took my temperature… she nearly threw a fit. Then, she checked my Hickman line and saw the traces of blood in the tube. I never even got upstairs.'

'You're joking?'

'Well, she did give me five minutes to collect a few bits from my room. My mum really gets panicky.'

'You haven't seen mine. She's always saying *'I'm not a trained nurse'.*

She couldn't stand flushing my line when I was first diagnosed.'

'How about your father? Doesn't he help?'

'My dad won't touch it. He always faints at the sight of a needle. My poor old mum had to learn; she had no choice. Nowadays we flush the line together. I hold the wiggly end and Mum puts the needle in the centre. Oh, I just remembered, I made up a new word while you were away.'

'What was that?'

'*Jamesless*. But I didn't need it.'

'Yes, it was a complete waste of time me going home, I didn't even have time to stroke the cats!'

'You and your cats! Oh, by the way, I opened your envelope.'

'That's not fair, I'm back. You didn't need to open it.'

'I'm glad I opened it. At last I know how you really feel. Oh James, let's try the touching hands through the glass like you said we would.'

She got up from the bed, being careful not to dislodge any of the tubes that connected her to the saline drip. She wobbled to the window pulling her drugs trolley behind her. She spread her fingers out wide and placed her hand against the window pane. He watched her and then, one by one, he touched each of her fingers with his hand through the cold glass. It was the way he had described holding her hand in his letter. Gwenny completely forgot her sickness for a moment and began thinking of the words for her next poem… *Finger by finger, digit by digit, you touch my hand…*

LOVE

The nurses will catch us,' he warned.

'So what? Everyone seems to know about us. Everyone…that is, except for your mum.'

'She knows now. I told her on the journey home.'

'What did she say?'

'She was glad I had found a friend on the ward.'

'You didn't say girlfriend then?'

'Let's take one step at time. You don't know my mum. Speak of the devil… I can see her talking to a nurse. I'd better go.' He took his hand away but Gwenny wanted to hold on to the moment.

'James, please don't go. You've only just come back.'

'Okay, I suppose I can stay a few more minutes. How many poems have you written?'

'Well, yesterday I was writing all about being *Jamesless* but now you're back so… I think I'll leave that one.'

'You could let me read it then I'll know the depth of your love.'

'*Depth of your love*. I love that phrase, it could be the title for a new poem.'

'Hey, Gwenny Evans, are you trying to steal the words out of my mouth?'

'You don't need them. I do.'

'Okay, so here's the deal. I'll let you have my title as long as you let me read the poem on your bed right now.'

He pointed to the papers on the bed and waited for her reply. She laughed. 'You sure you want to read that one, it's only a first draft?'

'Yes? That one… there. What's it about?'

'Nose bleeds!'

He laughed but Gwenny insisted on reading it out to him anyway…

Nosebleeds

Nosebleeds happen in a flash.

I never know when they are going to start

But when it does my nose feels all clogged up and I can't breathe properly.

I can almost taste the blood from my nostrils...

Nosebleeds just slip down the back of my throat

I feel like I am going to throw up,

The nurses and doctors try prodding and poking and pinching my nose.

They bring tissues that turn red,

They try ice cubes but still the bleeding won't stop.

Nosebleeds have a mind of their own,

They are most inconsiderate

They drip on my clothes and mess up my bed

They ruin lots of my mealtimes,

They make me go all red and blotchy,

Nosebleeds have become part of my daily life now,

But I will never get used to them,

I hate nosebleeds and especially when they have to be cauterized.

Yuk!

cHAPTER sEVENTEEN – gROWING pAINS

mISKIN hOUSE, sEVEN sISTERS (1972)

Gwenny was feeling very bloated and she didn't know why. Her stomach ached and she felt very uncomfortable. Also, she wasn't just tired, she was really worn out. Mum said it was growing pains and had gone ahead to arrange for Gwenny's fitting for her school gym tunic at the dressmaker's house. Gwenny was worried in case it was the wrong style. She didn't want to be the odd one out in her new school. She desperately wanted to have the same uniform as everyone else. But Gwenny's father was adamant that having the gym tunic made by the school outfitters was too expensive. He had told Mum to find a local dressmaker that would make it for half the cost. Gwenny hoped the dressmaker would not make her take her clothes off like last time. Gwenny liked to hide her body under big baggy clothes. She was beginning to develop a womanly body and she was very concious of her new curves.

'Gwenny,' called Mum, 'it's time to go to the dressmaker's house.'

'Coming Mum,' answered Gwenny, 'I have to go to the toilet first but I'll be there in minute.'

It was a very hot August day. Gwenny's clothes seemed to stick to her body and she noticed that there was a strong smell of underarm odour so she squirted on her anti-perspirant. When Gwenny went to the toilet she saw there were some brown stains on the gusset of her pants. So she wiped herself carefully with toilet paper, but as soon as she did this, she noticed a bright red stain on the white paper. *Oh my God. I am bleeding to death. I'm going to die,* she thought.

Gwenny had no idea that she had started her periods because no one had told her anything about it, so she shoved a big wad of toilet paper in her pants and hoped it would be alright until she got back from the dressmaker's house. She had already been measured for her gym tunic, but this time she would insist on trying the tunic on in the private. There was no way she was going to let the dressmaker see the big wad of toilet paper that she'd placed in her pants.

Thankfully the tunic was fine and only needed a few minor alterations.

'Good luck in grammar school.' said the dressmaker. 'When does the term start?'

'Next Monday,' answered Gwenny, and suddenly her stomach went all queasy as she thought *What if I'm still bleeding? Will I be able to go to grammar school?*

On the way home, Mum and Gwenny stopped at Clemmie's house to collect the younger children. Gwenny temporarily forgot her concerns when Clemmie opened the door holding a giant *Smartie* tube.

He gave the tube to Gwenny and exclaimed,

'Well done, Gwenny. You passed your eleven plus so here's your present, just as I promised.'

Gwenny took the tube and shook it hard. It rattled with coins. Then, she removed the end of the tube and all the coins tipped out onto the table.

'I told you I would save them for you,' said Clemmie, as he watched Gwenny empty the tube.

'Clemmie,' admonished Mum crossly. 'You've given Gwenny enough.You always give her a few pennies for going to the cafe to get your cigarettes.'

'Ah, but this is different. Gwenny earned this by working hard to pass her arithmetic. I promised her that if she passed the eleven plus she would have all the coins in the tube. Don't worry the others will have the same when their time comes.'

'But Clemmie,' said Mum. 'It's not that we don't appreciate what you give to the children, but there's over five pounds there. Are you sure you can afford it?'

'Your children are like my own grandchildren. Please let me decide what I can afford.'

Gwenny was delighted. In fact, as she counted the silver coins, she forgot all about her worries; that was until she got home; then all her fears returned when she went to the toilet and the pad of paper was still blood stained. She thought about it long and hard and she decided that if she was still bleeding in the morning she would tell her mum. Gwenny got up to go to the toilet many times that night. She was so worried that she would bleed all over her bed. In the morning, she was relieved to find that the sheets were unmarked, but there was a very bad 'growing pain' in her stomach. There was no time to delay, she would have to tell her mum. She waited for Mum to go upstairs to make the beds. Mum's routine was to change the beds every weekend so that they would be ready for the washing on a Monday morning. Mum always loved a little bit of help with the beds. To save on washing, Mum topped and tailed the beds. She placed a flat sheet from the top onto the mattress at the bottom, then she would put a clean sheet on the top. They were just changing the first bed when Gwenny blurted out, 'There was blood on my pants this morning.'

Mum, who had been preoccupied with changing the sheets, suddenly stopped. 'Oh Gwenny, you've started your periods,' said Mum, as she walked over to Gwenny's side of the bed and put her arm around Gwenny's shoulders. Gwenny immediately started to cry.

'I'm frightened Mum.'

'There's no need to be frightened Gwenny. It means you are growing up and becoming a woman.'

'I don't want to become a woman. I want to stay a little girl.'

'Oh, it's all right love. We'll find you a belt and some towels.'

'Why do I need a belt and a towel?' asked Gwenny, feeling confused by what Mum had said.

'Well Gwenny bach, the bleeding is going to last a few days. I'm so sorry that I didn't tell you about this before, but I thought you were too young to start your periods. You're not even twelve yet. But don't worry, everyone's different. I'll just get Beth to lend you some things until I have a chance to go to the chemist.'

Mum went downstairs and Gwenny sat on her bed. She felt very unhappy and confused as she had no idea what was happening to her. A few minutes later Beth came into Gwenny's room. Gwenny was lying on the freshly made bed.

'You've started then,' she mocked. 'No one starts their periods at eleven; trust you to be different.'

'Beth, please don't,' cried Gwenny. 'I don't understand what's happening.'

'Well, you're even more stupid than I thought you were. Everyone knows about periods. Trust me to have a stupid sister.'

She threw a white elasticated sanitary belt onto Gwenny's bed.

'Keep it, I don't want it back.'

Then, she opened a bag and took out a small booklet entitled *All you need to know about your period.*

'Mum said to give you this. It tells you that your periods will happen for the next forty years.'

Gwenny watched as her sister walked out of the door. She looked at her own reflection in the mirror. Her face stared back white and pale. She didn't like the sound of this going on for forty years.

Was she going to be bleeding all the time?

Gwenny sat on the bed and read about periods. She was aghast that they would happen once a month for the rest of her life. Nobody had warned her of this. How dare Mum and Beth know all about periods. She was annoyed that they had treated her like a baby and hadn't told her anything.

Gwenny lay on her bed reading until Mum came in and showed her how to put on the sanitary belt. She helped Gwenny attach the loops of the towel onto the hooks. Gwenny found it all very complicated. She also felt very uncomfortable. In fact, she was very conscious that she was all padded up like a big, fat sandwich. *This would take a lot of getting used to,* she thought. She felt that everyone would know she was having a period because the sanitary towel seemed to jut out through her clothes, but Mum reassured her that no one else would know it was there. Suddenly, Gwenny felt frightened. Did this mean that she couldn't play with her little brother and sister again? Was she now too grown up to play with *Bayko* and the wooden blocks? She hated all this grown up business. She was only eleven years old, she wasn't ready to be a woman…not yet!

The next morning Gwenny woke up with a start. The alarm was ringing. The shrill sound pierced her eardrums as she opened her eyes. She had dreamt that she was bleeding to death. There had been blood pouring out of her mouth, her nose, her eyes and every orifice of her body. The blood had stained her new gym tunic and saturated her bedding. And, even more strangely, she was lying in a bed surrounded by hundreds of coins.

cHAPTER eIGHTEEN - oUT oF iSOLATION

cHILDREN'S cANCER wARD, sOUTHAMPTON (1976)

'Don't push me! Please don't hurt me,' Gwenny cried out.

'It's alright Gwenny. I'm here,' reassured Mum.

Gwenny screamed again and with her eyes tightly closed she lashed out as if she was defending herself from an attack.

'It's only a dream Gwenny. Only a dream,' repeated Mum soothingly.

Gwenny opened her eyes wide and stared at her mum as if she were the crazy one.

'It's me, Gwenny.'

'She was threatening me. She was getting me back for not waiting for her.'

'Hush now… you're okay. But who was threatening you in that dream?'

'It was that Daisy Bishop and her cronies in school. It was so vivid I thought it was really happening,' exclaimed Gwenny, rubbing her eyes.

'But it's not real,' Mum paused. 'Or is it?'

Gwenny did not reply.

'What's up? You looked absolutely terrified when you opened your eyes. It's time to tell me, Gwenny. I need to know the truth.'

'It happened,' admitted Gwenny, with her head bent down avoiding eye contact with her mum. 'They used to threaten me at school.'

She grabbed a tissue from the box on her bedside cabinet.

'Threaten you! Why didn't you tell anybody?'

'I kept thinking they would stop,' Gwenny sniffled.

'But Gwenny, no one is allowed to treat another person like that. You are not going back to that school.'

'Can I go to a new school, Mum?' asked Gwenny, her face suddenly lighting up. 'Do you really mean it?'

'What did they actually do to you?'

'They did loads of things but you don't want to know…it was so humiliating.'

'Humiliating or not. I **do** want to know.'

'Well, they locked me in the P.E. cupboard for a whole lunchtime and they threatened that if I told on them they would do worse things. So I didn't tell on them and ended up getting a detention for missing lessons.'

'Was there anything else, Gwenny? I need to know the truth if the head teacher is going to allow you move schools.'

Gwenny would have loved to have had the courage to tell her mum everything but somehow she just couldn't. What would her dad do if he knew that those girls had pushed her into a toilet cubicle and shoved her head down the toilet pan? She cringed as she remembered the flush of the water on her face and the chemical stench of the toilet pan. She couldn't tell her parents. Her dad would go straight up the school and he wouldn't stop at just telling them off. So instead she said, 'Well, there was lots of name calling and pinching my bus pass. At first, I thought it was me losing my things, but then I lost my dinner money and my book of poems and each time I got into trouble with the teachers.'

Tears welled up in Mum's eyes as she pulled Gwenny closer.

'Oh Gwenny bach, those girls were bullying you. They'll choose another victim now that you're not there. It can't be allowed to continue. I'll make an appointment to see the head teacher as soon as possible. But Gwenny, why didn't you tell us?'

'I was feeling ill, so tired all the time.'

'What about the dreams? How often are you having these nightmares?'

'Not many recently. Not since I met James.'

'And are these the *'so-called friends'* who bought you the portable TV?'

'Yeah. They probably felt guilty when they found out I'd got cancer.'

'Oh… Gwenny…you poor little thing. Why do these things always happen to you?'

<u>Sunday, February 29 (9.00 a.m.)</u>

I had one of my nightmares. It was all about that bitch Daisy again. Rosie and I were going into town after school when Daisy came up to us at the end of our P.E. lesson and said, 'Can I come into town with you? I'll just go and change into my uniform and I'll be with you in just a sec.'

Rosie and I looked at each other in astonishment. Daisy was asking to come into town with us?

'We're going to the Wimpy Bar.' I said firmly. 'You're not invited.'

I was really proud of myself for saying that. It's strange how I never stand up for myself in reality and yet in a dream I can hear myself saying all the right things. Then, in my dream, Daisy changed out of her school uniform but we didn't wait for her. After that the rest of the dream was a bit of a blur until Daisy walked into the Wimpy bar and came to sit on our table. She picked up a menu and held it in front of her face. She pretended she was choosing what to order. But instead of ordering a meal she snarled at us from behind the menu, 'I'll get you back for not waiting for me. You can't mess around with Daisy Bishop.'

At that point, the dream ended and I woke up screaming. I'm still shaking even now after that awful nightmare. I know that it was only a dream but I think that it was meant to happen when my mum was here because now she knows all about the bullying and I won't ever have to go back to that horrid school again. It's funny how weird dreams can be. Why would Daisy want to go to the Wimpy bar with me and Rosie when she always has her bunch of cronies around her? I hate dreams. Since I've been in hospital, the only ones I remember are the nightmares.

Gwenny crossed another day off her calendar and then she unlocked her dairy with the little key.

Monday March 1 (9.00 a.m.)

Today is the day I am allowed out of isolation. Hurrah! For once I don't know what to write because I simply can't wait for Dr Neville's round. He is supposed to give me the thumbs up. I hope he will bring me good news. I don't know what I will do if not. I told him I would leave anyway. He said if I misbehaved he'd keep me here for another six weeks... Please, oh, please God, let me be able to leave this room today.

Gwenny opened the door of her room by herself and with her mum at her side she took her first steps into the ante room where the overalls, masks and gloves were kept for the isolation cubicle. She couldn't believe the relief she felt as she stepped into the unfamiliar room. She took a deep breath and then, as she opened the second door which led to the corridor, she stopped in amazement as she was greeted by a group of people standing outside her door.

'Three cheers for Gwenny,' shouted Jackie. The sheer voloume of the cheers made Gwenny shrink back into her mum's arms. She was secretly thrilled with the greeting party, but she had a very uneasy feeling in her tummy. She hadn't been around that many people for a very long time and she couldn't help noticing all the different smells; no longer the clean, antiseptic fragrance of her little room, but the lingering scent of burnt toast and smelly armpits. *It's funny*, she thought to herself, *I'd actually forgotten these smells existed.* She was also overwhelmed by the clapping as she held tightly on to her mum. Her legs felt wobbly and jelly-like.

'Mum, I really need to sit down,' whispered Gwenny.

Mum guided her gently to the nearest chair.

'Well done, Gwenny. You've made it back into the real world again,' called out Jackie. 'We thought we'd give you a surprise, so close your eyes.'

Gwenny closed her eyes tightly and listened to the shuffling of feet. When she opened her eyes, there in front of her stood all the members of her family; Dad, Clemmie, Beth, Rosie and even her little brother Gareth. They had all been hiding behind the crowd and were now standing in front of the group. The whole family had come to the hospital to celebrate Gwenny coming out of isolation.

'I don't know what to say?' she exclaimed, as they all surrounded her chair.

'That's a first,' cheered Clemmie. 'Our Gwenny is lost for words. It's going to be a quiet day.'

Everyone laughed.

'Let's give the family a little space,' said Jackie thoughtfully. 'You can all go in the school room for a little tea party. I've prepared some food for you.'

As they walked towards the school room, Gwenny could hear her mum saying to Clemmie, 'I never thought I'd see this day. It's been a long time coming.'

'I'm so proud of her,' She heard Clemmie answer.

They all had their lunch together around the big school table. Gwenny was delighted that all the foods that she hadn't been allowed in isolation were now back on the menu. She even had a cracker with pate and a little soft cheese in a sandwich. It felt like Christmas. Rosie entertained them all with a solo on her flute and Gareth had brought his latest football trophies to show Gwenny. Even Beth came to sit next to her and asked how she was feeling. At one point, Dad almost hugged her but changed his mind at the very last minute. He said that he was afraid of transferring germs, but Gwenny knew how hard it was for her dad to show any kind of affection. The family finished all the food and then Gwenny's nurse came to the schoolroom and announced, 'That's enough visiting for one day. You can all visit again tomorrow.' Then, she turned to Gwenny and said, 'I'll be back in a few minutes with your medicines, young lady.'

After saying goodbye to the family, Mum said she had to go and make a few phonecalls and so Gwenny walked through the inter-connecting door into the empty parents' lounge. The large screen television was on but Gwenny was glad to be alone. She stood with her back to the school room door and listened to the news until the door from the corridor opened. She watched somewhat puzzled as a tall, slim figure entered the room. He was wearing a green gown, a hat to cover his hair and a white mask over his mouth, but she knew those blue eyes anywhere. It was as if the world stood still as he removed the mask to reveal his face.

'James, James,' Gwenny repeated as she rushed into his arms. 'I can't believe you are really here.'

'Hello, Gwenny Evans,' James grinned, 'I didn't realise you were so small.'

He looked at her face and then gently guided her across the room to the sofa. There was a strong smell of cigarettes coming from an ashtray on the coffee table, but Gwenny ignored it as they sat on the sofa side by side

'Gwenny Evans, how do you do?' said James, picking up her hand and pretending to shake it. 'You are even more beautiful now that I'm sitting next to you.'

'I can't believe I'm here. I can't believe I'm out of isolation at last.'

She felt her senses would explode as her nose and ears were filled with the unfamiliar touch and smell of James!

'James is it ok if we have a *cwtch*?'

'Let me just check that again. I need to know what I'm agreeing to. What's a *cwtch*?'

'It's the welsh word for a hug. I'll show you.'

A few minutes later Gwenny sighed contentedly.

'Good *cwtch*?' checked James.

'The best,' sighed Gwenny.'James, I'll have to get used to actually being with you. Do you know what I mean? '

'Yeah, I must admit I was feeling a bit scared too, but remember we have all the time in the world.'

'But I want to know…' she started.

'Hush,' he said, as he gently put his arm around her shoulder.

'How you feel about me?' she continued.

'What do you mean? How do I feel? How am I supposed to feel?'

'Do you still like me? Now that you've met me.'

'Yes. I could eat you up,' he whispered in her ear.

'There'll be no eating up,' she laughed.

'Just to cwtch you is enough.We'll take it one step at a time.'

'Thank you James, don't ever let me go.'

'I won't ever let you go. My beautiful, gorgeous Gwenny Evans, Miskin House, Seven Sisters.' James sighed as they held each other tightly.

Gwenny broke the silence and asked. 'Why did you say my name and the name of my first home in Wales just then.'

'Well, just at that moment I remembered you telling me the story of your little budgie, who chirped his name and address *Bobby Evans, Miskin House, Seven Sisters* and I suddenly thought *Gwenny Evans, Miskin House, Seven Sisters*... You're just like a little bird… so tiny… so delicate…so precious… my little Miskin girl.'

cHAPTER nINETEEN - gRAMMAR sCHOOL

sEVEN sISTERS (1972)

'You don't look like Gwenny anymore,' stated Gareth rather sadly.

'Who do I look like then?' asked Gwenny.

'You look like a proper school girl. You look just like Beth.'

'She's bound to look like Beth. She's wearing all Beth's old school uniform,' chipped in Rosie.

'Ugh, I bet it smells,' exclaimed Gareth, pretending to hold his nose.

'What's that? Who smells?' asked Mum, as she and Clemmie walked into the kitchen where the three children were having their breakfast.

'Gwenny, don't listen to them. The uniform doesn't smell and you look clean and tidy doesn't she Clemmie?,' stated Mum, turning to Clemmie.

'You look very grown up Gwenny,' agreed Clemmie, 'you should be very proud of your uniform because you worked really hard to get to grammar school.'

'But Clemmie, I don't want to go. I'm too scared,' said Gwenny, rushing into his arms.

'I know how you're feeling Gwenny, but we're all a little bit scared of new things. Look at your mum. She's starting her teacher training course today and I bet she's feeling a little bit worried too.'

'I'm feeling very apprehensive,' admitted Mum. 'But at least I don't have to worry about all of you because Clemmie will be here every morning. He's also going to be here after school today so you can have your tea before I get home.

'Oh Mum, it will be so different. You'll be going to college and I'll be going to school in Neath.'

'I know it won't be the same, but once I get my timetable, there'll be some mornings when I can give you and Beth a lift to school. Like today, I don't have to be at college till after nine, so you and Beth can have a lift with me in the car. We're so lucky that my college is only down the road from the grammar school.'

Gwenny walked over to her mum and hugged her.

'Right Gwenny, when you've finished your breakfast you need to go upstairs quietly because your dad's asleep. Your P.E. kit and your books are ready on the ottoman, you only have to check your things and pack everything in your satchel.'

Gwenny tiptoed up the stairs to her room as she didn't want to wake her dad, who had been working a night shift. She checked her watch; she still had a few minutes before she had to be at the bus stop. She picked up her favourite pen and started to write.

Monday, September 4 - (7.45 a.m.)

Today's my first day in grammar school. They say that on the first day all the first formers have their heads put down the toilet pan! They say the prefects give first formers lines if they are caught running in the corridors! They say first formers get one hundred lines if they forget to wear the beret. I hope they won't know I'm a first former. I would die if I have to write hundred lines. I think my arm would drop off. The teachers in grammar school have weird names like Enfys Buns. I wonder if she likes buns, or does she wear her hair in a bun? Then, there is the head teacher, who they all call Maud. Her name is Miss Morgan and if you need a pass to go into town at lunch time, you have to ask her permission at morning play time. I don't think I will ever go into town because I'd never have the courage to ask for a pass. Oh, why does the grammar school have to be so different? I loved my old junior school. I wish I was still there with Rosie. I knew all the teachers in my old school and I used to feel safe and happy there. In grammar school there won't be any boys in my class. The boys' school is across the stream and you're not allowed to talk to the boys during playtime or at dinner times. There are so many rules and regulations. I am sure I'll get things wrong. Mum says I'll be okay but I am not convinced. Beth won't tell me anything because she says she had to find out for herself. She says I am such a baby. I wish I wasn't going to grammar school. I know I'm going to ***HATE*** *it there.*

Gwenny actually had a very uneventful first day at grammar school; no one was nasty to her and everything was fine until home time when she realised she didn't know where to catch the bus to go home. Gwenny had been dropped off at the school gates by her mum in the morning, and, although she had been on the tour of the school, no one had actually told her where to catch the bus home. Unfortunately, she was one of the last girls in the cloakroom and when she eventually got to the canteen car park, where the buses parked, most of the buses had already left. Gwenny panicked as she suddenly realised she had no idea what number bus would take her home.

She returned to her classroom to ask her teacher to help her but all the first form classrooms were empty. She thought she would go to the staffroom and knock on the door. But on the way there she bumped into the formidable Miss Morgan. The one they all called Maud! She knew it was Miss Morgan because she had seen her standing on the hall stage that morning in assembly. She had seemed distant and remote then but now standing next to the tall, heavily built woman. Gwenny felt very small and helpless.

'Sorry,' she muttered as she bumped into the head teacher, who was coming out of her study.

'And who are you?' said Miss Morgan in a slow, disgusted tone.

'I'm Gwenny Evans,' answered Gwenny, struggling to stand upright due to the weight of her books in her new leather satchel.

'What form are you in?' enquired Miss Morgan.

'1B.'

'1B. Miss Morgan, if you please.'

'Sorry. 1B… Miss Morgan.' stuttered Gwenny, blushing.

'So… Gwenny Evans. Could you tell me why you are still at school when the school buses left ten minutes ago?'

'I didn't know where the buses went from, and then when I did find the car park I didn't know which number bus to get,' mumbled Gwenny, struggling to get her words out. 'And… and…by then… my…my bus had already gone.'

'Have you a tongue, Gwenny Evans?'

'Yes, Miss Morgan,' answered Gwenny, poking her tongue out obligingly.

'Well, why don't you use it to speak properly?'

'I don't know Miss Morgan.'

'You don't know?' she paused. 'Where do you live Gwenny Evans? Or is that something else you don't know?'

'Miskin house, Miss Morgan.'

'And where might that be?'

'It's Miskin house, Seven Sisters, Miss Miskin,' Gwenny paused and tried again.

'Sorry, Miss…Miss..Mmm… Morgan,' stuttered Gwenny.

'My, what a tongue twister that was. Well, Gwenny Evans from Miskin House, Seven Sisters. How are you going to get home? It's a long way, probably nine miles; you can't possibly walk.'

'Well, my mum is training to be a teacher. She's at the college down the road today, Miss Morgan.'

'In that case, I'll get my secretary to ring the college and ask for your mum to pick you up on her way home. Meanwhile, Gwenny Evans, you'll write fifty lines. *I will not miss my bus at the end of the school day.*'

Several minutes later, Gwenny thought her hand would drop off as she sat in the secretary's office. She had been told to stay there until she finished her lines. Her mum had been contacted and she would pick Gwenny up in about half an hour. As she sat there she watched the secretary turn the handle of the Banda machine. She had never seen a machine like it before. It intrigued her the way that it produced sheets of purple print just by turning the handle. Gwenny noticed that there was a strong smell. She sniffed and sneezed several times.

'It's the duplicator fluid,' explained the secretary. 'Everyone comments on how strong the smell is. I'm so used to it… I don't notice it anymore.'

Then the secretary continued turning the handle of the machine that churned out sheet after sheet of purple print. Gwenny watched fascinated as each printed sheet of paper landed on the extended tray. It reminded her so much of Dad's printing press.

Later, on the way home in the car, Gwenny promised herself that one day she would produce a book of poems with not just purple print, but a book which used all different types of print. Print that could be produced in every colour of the rainbow.

cHAPTER tWENTY – iNTO pRINT

cHILDREN'S cANCER wARD, sOUTHAMPTON (1976)

Gwenny wanted her book to be ring bound using a variety of different fonts and interspersed with lots of illustrations. She wanted the book to be divided into colour zones of feelings. For example, yellow pages for happiness, blue for sadness, green for calm and red for anger. She wanted a book that had pages with pockets and flaps for tiny things to be kept in. Gwenny's ideas rolled off her tongue as Tim, who worked for dad's printing firm, shook his head in despair.

'Oh well,' said Gwenny looking at Jackie. 'One day I will make a book of poems to evoke all my senses. I'll have pages with pockets of smells, bizarre buttons, silver keys for tiny padlocks, magic pebbles, pipe cleaners to make dream catchers and… and…'

'Okay, we get the idea, but right now it's all about getting your book printed ready for your book launch,' said Tim, smiling but in a serious tone.

'I'm having a book launch?' Gwenny questioned, looking to Jackie for an answer.

'Yes, you are. We're going to invite 'Hampshire Cancer Charity' and all the local dignitaries to the book launch so we can start selling your book that day. We can assume that everyone, who supports the local charity will be buying at least one copy of your book. They will also be making donations so that will guarantee the fundraising will get off to a flying start.'

'I can't believe it.' Gwenny gasped. 'It's going to be just like being the author of a proper book. Oh Jackie, how did you manage to arrange it?'

'Well, with a lot of help from a typist and your dad's printing firm actually.'

'What about the illustrations?'

'Ah, we have a surprise for you Gwenny,' replied Jackie and she stepped outside the school room. She returned a minute later with James.

'James? Why are you here?' asked Gwenny smiling.

'I'm your illustrator,' answered James.

'What…and you never told me.'

'I had to keep it a secret… didn't I Jackie?'

'Yes, James has been secretly working with me and I asked him to keep it as a surprise. He's a very good artist,' declared Jackie. 'You should see how he's illustrated the printing press poem.'

Jackie went through her file and handed Gwenny an A4 piece of paper.

'Oh James,' praised Gwenny. 'You must have listened to every word I said about my father's printing press. It's a really good illustration. For a minute then I thought I was back in my father's printing shed.'

'Well, James did talk to your father too,' Jackie interrupted.

'So everyone knew all about this except for me?'

'Well, we had to do something while you were lazing around in the isolation ward,' piped up James.

'I can't believe all this. It's the best present I've ever had,' exclaimed Gwenny.

'Well, young lady,' said Tim. 'Never mind about the best present you have ever had. Let's get back to what we were talking about, if this young man is the illustrator, perhaps he can help us. By the way, have you got a title for the book?'

'I'm thinking of calling it *Rainbows* because rainbows are a symbol of hope for the future.'

'Yes, I think that's a brilliant title, but it's got to be in black and white because we've got to keep the costs low. How are we going to illustrate the rainbow?'

'Maybe James has got some ideas?' suggested Jackie hopefully.

James looked at Gwenny, 'May I make a suggestion? I could make a drawing of a rainbow with two fluffy clouds at either end. Then, I could write in black ink all the words we need for our cover page inside the first cloud.'

'Brilliant...What do you think Gwenny?' asked Tim.

'I like it and perhaps we could even put some lines from a poem inside the other cloud.'

'Sounds like my job's going to be easy; you two have all the ideas. So I'll put together a first draft and once we've got it all typed and proof read, we'll print it at Miskin Printers; so we should be ready for the book launch in a few weeks time.'

Tim paused and looked over at Jackie thoughtfully.

'Jackie, have you booked the date and the venue?' asked Tim.

'Yes, I've arranged it for Wednesday, March 16 in the afternoon. We can't change it as the hospital training suite is all booked up,' answered Jackie.

'And how many people can we expect?'

'Fifty to sixty people I believe. The invitations are ready to go out and posters are going to be displayed all over the hospital this week.'

'Jackie, you've worked hard.'

'Not as hard as Gwenny. She had to write all the poems and get better at the same time.'

'This book is going to be an excellent fundraiser for the ward. Have you ever done anything like this before?' enquired Tim.

'No, we've never had a poet on the ward before,' replied Jackie looking at

Gwenny.

'It's going to make such a difference to the lives of teenagers, who have cancer in the future. That's the most important thing,' stated Gwenny.

'Well spoken, Gwenny,' said Tim, 'you keep those words for your interview with the press. They absolutely love people, who do things to help others.'

Later at the photo session.

'Could you move your arm a little this way?' asked Sam, the photographer.

Gwenny moved her arm as requested.

'Yes, that's perfect. Big smile and…hold that pose.'

Gwenny smiled.

'Smile again Gwenny. Look at your mum and smile. Brilliant! These shots will be great.'

There was a slight pause as the photographer checked his camera and then he said, 'Could we have the next shot sitting on your bed? How about if we have your books strewn everywhere… yeah…like that all over the bed. Can you put out all your notebooks, dictionaries and pieces of paper. I want your room to look like you are a writer.'

'I am a writer.'

'Yeah…sorry. I didn't mean it like that. Of course, you're a writer, but we only have space for the best shots in the magazine so each photo has to tell a story.'

'Do I wear my wig or not?' asked Gwenny.

The photographer looked at his colleague.

'We would like to try one shot without your wig. But if you're not comfortable…we understand.'

'I'm fine without my wig, what do you think Mum?'

Mum nodded in agreement.

There was a moment of hesitation and then the female journalist said. 'Well, if you're sure you don't mind?'

'No, my hair is growing back now so I'm not completely bald.'

'Okay, so can you wear something pink and feminine?'

'Well, I've got my pink fluffy dressing gown.'

'Yeah, that's great. Just pop the dressing gown over your top and sit on the bed like this.'

He showed her how to sit by actually positioning himself on the bed.

'Nurse,' Sam called out. 'Can you stand in the background? Can you pretend you're connecting Gwenny to her drugs trolley? Can you hold a saline bag, or whatever they call it?'

'Just coming,' answered Gwenny's nurse.

'Yes, that's fine,' Sam said to the nurse a few minutes later. 'You're just in the back of the photo. Perfect.'

'So will this be the last photo?' asked Gwenny.

'Yes. Sorry we've taken so long, but these shots have to be spot on for our features editor or she won't even run your story.'

Monday, March 8 (4.00 p.m.)

I really enjoyed the photo shoot but it didn't half take forever. I absolutely loved having a proper make up artist to myself. She arrived after lunch and laid out a whole stack of make up brushes. I've never seen so many brushes! She had one brush for this and one for that. She did my make up very naturally and I loved the way she made up my eyes. Sam chose to do one shot in the schoolroom. He asked Jackie if he could rearrange the furniture to get the best light. Then, he put up a silver umbrella thing to deflect the light, or whatever.

Sam decided he wanted a photo of me and my mum reading a poem together, and while he was setting up that shot Maggie, the journalist, asked me some questions about myself, my family, my illness and my treatment. My mum stayed with me in case I didn't know what to say, but I have plenty to say about the children's cancer ward. I felt like a pop star with all the attention I got. It's not every day a girl gets the opportunity to appear in a teen magazine. I was even given time to read back what the reporter had written, but it was mostly in shorthand. In the end, she had to read it back to me and I had to nod my head, or say if I didn't like it. But who am I to argue with a journalist from London? It all sounded brilliant to me, a bit exaggerated maybe, but they have to sensationalise the story to capture the reader's interest. Well, at least that's what she told me. I have really loved every minute of my day. In fact, I know for certain that I want to be a journalist when I leave school.

cHAPTER tWENTY-oNE - qUEENIE'S pARLOUR sHOP

sEVEN sISTERS (1972)

'Mum, Gwenny wants to be a journalist but she won't tell me what a journalist is.'

'Be quiet Rosie. I'll tell you later.'

'I won't be quiet. I want to know now,' insisted Rosie.

'Well it's a ....sort of...,' started Mum.

'Don't tell her,' Gwenny interrupted. 'Rosie always wants to be the same as me.'

'No, I don't... you're the one who's always copying,' insisted Rosie. 'You had the same breakfast cereal as me this morning.'

'I always have porridge...Mum don't I always have porridge?' pleaded Gwenny.

'Yes you do, but usually with hot milk. Today you had cold milk.'

'That's because all the hot milk had skin on top of it. I hate skin!'

'Beth took all the hot milk and left the skin on top; that wasn't me,' Rosie continued

'You always take all the hot milk, Gwenny,' interrupted Beth.

'Beth stay out of it!' warned Mum. 'Girls...girls! I've had enough of your quarrelling. I need you to finish your breakfast in silence... now!'

The girls continued to eat their breakfast and for once they listened.

'Beth, I need you to go down to Queenie's shop to get some things for dinner,' announced Mum, a few minutes later. 'I need a loaf of bread, 3lb of potatoes, some crackers and cheese. You'd better take Gwenny with you. She can help you carry all the shopping.

'Oh Mummy, please can I go with them?' asked Rosie. 'I promise I'll hold

Beth's hand.'

'Actually,' said Mum, 'that's a good idea. It will give me the chance to get on with my jobs.'

Mum walked out to the scullery, where Beth was putting on her shoes and coat.

'Beth, can you take Gareth with you? You can put him in the pushchair and Rosie can hold onto the handles.'

'Well, I'd rather take Rosie than Gwenny.'

'No, that's not fair, you need to take Gwenny. She'll help you carry the shopping. Now here's the list and a purse.'

'Is there money for sweets?' asked Rosie eagerly, entering the room.

'You can have one penny each for sweets but I want change. Now let's get you all ready, I can't stand here all day just gossiping, I've got to get the baby dressed. Then, Dad needs me to help him in the printing shed."

'Mummy, can I have an ice lollipop in Queenie's shop?' begged Rosie.

'No, Rosie and that's my final answer. Don't ask for anything else.'

Ten minutes later Mum took the children outside to make sure that they crossed the main road safely.

'Mum, do I have to go?' asked Gwenny, dragging her feet and scraping the toes of her shoes on the stony pavement.

'Gwenny… shoes,' cautioned mum, pointing to Gwenny's feet. 'Yes… you do have to go. Beth needs your help with the younger ones, and make sure you hold Rosie's hand especially when you're walking along the main road.'

Ten minutes later they arrived at the parlour shop, and Beth undid the straps to get Gareth out of the pushchair while Gwenny read the sign on the door that said:-

Please ring the doorbell and step inside. I will be with you shortly.

Gwenny rang the bell and the four children trooped into the house, which looked like an ordinary house from the outside but was full of boxes and crates inside. The 'cardboard' smell of the shop greeted them as the children followed Beth into the converted front room. Behind the glass counter they could see Queenie's children. The boy was already calling to his mum; the girl tried to duck to hide her face but Gareth had already spotted her.

'Why has she got purple on her face?' asked Gareth loudly, pointing to the girl behind the counter.

'Shh…be quiet Gareth,' whispered Gwenny.

'I won't be quiet,' protested Gareth, 'It looks funny. Why don't she wash it off?'

'What sweets are you having Gareth?' asked Gwenny, trying to change the subject.

Just then Queenie came into the parlour shop. She was wiping her hands on a tea towel.

'Sorry,' she apologised, 'I was out the back in the wash house putting the clothes through the mangle. What can I get for you?'

'Mum has written a note,' explained Beth. She took the paper out of the purse and started reading out the list of items. Queenie and her son quickly filled the shopping basket. Then Queenie jotted down the prices so she could add them up.

'Is that all?' she asked, looking at Beth.

'Mummy said we can all have sweets,' chirped Rosie.

'Yes, but only a pennyworth,' reminded Beth.

Rosie and Gareth were standing in front of the sweets counter. They were gazing longingly at the boxes and jars overflowing with pink shrimps, white mice, sweet cigarettes and a selection of chocolate bars.

'I want four fruit salads and a white mouse,' demanded Rosie.

'Me too,' copied Gareth.

'You can't have all those,' said Beth crossly.

'They can have my white mice,' offered Gwenny, 'they're two for one penny.'

'You're far too soft with them,' admonished Beth, sounding like their father.

Beth paid for the sweets. She thanked Queenie for the shopping. Then she took both Rosie and Gareth outside to the pushchair. She squeezed them both into the large seat, leaving Gwenny to bring all the shopping.

'Beth, Beth… don't leave me behind,' moaned Gwenny.

'You're such a slow coach, Gwenny. You can't even run to save your life. Ha! ha!' laughed Beth as she raced off with the push chair.

'Faster, faster,' squealed Rosie in delight, as she held onto the bar of the pushchair.

'Faster, faster,' echoed Gareth.

Later that day Gwenny spoke to Mum about what had happened in the shop.

'Mum, we saw the girl with the purple birthmark today.'

'Oh, yes…you mean Queenie's daughter, Arwen? She's a lovely little girl.'

'Mum, have you ever seen her face?'

'Yes, but it's not nice to stare.'

'Why was she born like that?'

'I don't know but I do know that her mum and dad love her very much. They do their best to try and protect her from other people's nasty remarks. She doesn't go to school very often as she's always in and out hospital. She also had polio when she was little and so she spends a lot of her time at home.'

'But, Gwenny…why all these questions? You've seen Rhiannon in chapel with her family. They always sit in the back pew when she's with them.'

'Oh Mum, I felt so awful when Gareth shouted, ***'Why has that girl got a purple face?'***

'Gareth is too young to understand what he's saying. But I hope you and Beth didn't allow him to carry on shouting.'

'No, I tried to distract him by asking what sweets he wanted.'

'Well done Gwenny. I can always rely on you to be sensible.'

A few hours later, she wasn't feeling very sensible. She kept thinking about Arwen, her illness and the purple birthmark on her face.

'Mum, can I have some milk please?' asked Gwenny, 'I can't sleep. I feel so cold and I keep thinking about that poor little girl, Arwen.'

'Don't worry about the Arwen. Nothing like that will ever happen to you. You're so lucky with your pretty face and beautiful hair. Here's your hot water bottle so go back upstairs now. You'll soon go to sleep when you're warm and cosy in your own little bed.'

cHAPTER tWENTY-tWO – jOURNALS aND gAMES

cHILDREN'S cANCER wARD, sOUTHAMPTON (1976)

Tuesday, March 9 (9.00 a.m.)

Today I had the letter I had been half expecting. It was from the head teacher of my 'old' school. I am so glad I can call it my 'old' school because I need never go back there again. Mum went to see the head teacher, who made Daisy Bishop and her friends, write me a letter of apology for the way they treated me. The head teacher, in her letter, also apologised on behalf of the school and assured me that as a result of their unkind behaviour Daisy Bishop and her group of friends have been split up and they are now in different form groups. They are no longer allowed to mix each other in school and their parents have been informed.

Tuesday, March 9 (11.00 a.m.)

I'm balancing my typewriter on the bed table over my bed today to type my journal. I still like writing about things that make me laugh. On the way to my scan today, I saw a man's naked bottom. If I told Mum she would have a fit. If she'd seen me looking she would have been shocked. She would have said, "Avert your eyes" in a disapproving tone. But I am fifteen going on sixteen. The hospital should have zips up the back of the theatre gowns then everyone would be covered up. P.S. It was a hairy bum…ugh!

James and I played 'Hangman' today. He's really good at it. I wonder why he's so clever and I'm not? After finishing 'Hangman' we played a game of 'Boy, girl, animal, place.' I got the letter 'Q'. What sort of animal or creature begins with 'Q'? I suggested, 'Queen bee.' But James said I couldn't have that because queen bee should come under 'B'. It got us giggling again. I haven't laughed so much in ages. He teases me all the time with his funny comments.

Wednesday, March 10 (9.00 a.m.)

Today is "deep clean day" and I'm supposed to spend most of the morning out of my room. The cleaners are wiping down every surface; they are even cleaning the top of the curtain rail! I'm allowed outside the ward as long as I stay inside the hospital building. I'm supposed to let the nurses know where I am going though. I am looking forward to Clemmie's visit later today as Mum and Dad are at work.

Minutes later Clemmie walked into the school room.

'So what's new Gwenny? I've heard on the grapevine that I've been replaced by a younger model.'

Gwenny blushed, 'I could never replace you Clemmie.'

'Well, I'm getting worried,' announced Clemmie. 'Should I tell your mother to buy

a hat for the wedding?'

Gwenny smiled. 'James is soooooo lovely. I've told him so much about you. You two will get on really well. I really like him.'

'I know. You haven't talked about anyone else for ages.'

'He won't die… will he Clemmie?'

'I have no idea my love. Death is in God's hands… but I do know that you'll be better soon because you're responding so well to your treatment. So…this boy called James…is he your boyfriend then Gwenny?'

'I don't know yet but I would love him to be.'

'A word of warning Gwenny, be careful. All teenage boys get ideas.'

'It's not like that Clemmie,' answered Gwenny blushing.

'Well, you make sure you look after yourself.'

'I will,' she promised, 'What can we possibly get up to here in hospital?'

'You don't know young lads,' warned Clemmie.

<u>Wednesday, March 10 (4.00.p.m.)</u>

After a lovely afternoon, I've the headache from hell. The pain in my head is going right across my forehead. I keep putting my fingers on each side of my head to try and get some relief. This headache is the worst I have had for a long time. I'm really cheesed off with feeling so rough. The cardboard sick bowls are lined up ready just in case I need to vomit. James has drawn hearts and smiley faces on them in black felt tip pens. He's so funny. He does such crazy things. He is guaranteed to make me laugh even when I feel so ill.

Sorry diary…had to pause there to be sick and deal with yet another nosebleed. It's taken me ages to clean myself up. The sick came out with such a big whoosh… it even came down my nostrils. It made my throat feel all dry and scratchy. I think the vomit might have come out of my ears if it had lasted any longer. Then, without warning my nose started bleeding again. There was blood everywhere. I had to rush to the bathroom as I had run out of tissues. I will have to write a list of the things I need when Mum visits me later on.

<u>Thursday, March 11 (8.00.a.m.)</u>

Today I feel much better. I don't know what happened to me yesterday but at least I've stopped feeling sick and the headache has gone away. It's good timing because when I woke up this morning James's letter was waiting on my bedside cabinet. It said…

Dear Gwenny Evans, (alias Miskin Girl)

I have just listened to the weather focus for tonight. It is a clear night with a full moon. It is the perfect night to see the stars. I may even catch you a shooting star. If the coast is clear I will come to your room to wake you. But if not, meet me at the fire exit door at 10 pm. Wear warm clothes as we are going outside on the roof.

Love from James XXX

Inside my head, I began to chant he loves me, he loves me not, he loves me! He wrote me a letter and signed it 'Love from James.' My only problem at this moment is what to wear? My hair is growing back. Should I wear my wig or a hat? Should I wear a coat or a dressing gown? Should I wear my pyjamas or a jogging suit? There are so many decisions attached to going on a first date but not everyone shares a first date with cancer!

Thursday, March 11 (2.00.p.m.)

Today I told my nurse that I was going downstairs to the shop but instead I found myself getting out of the lift at floor five... I can't face stairs yet! Not on my own! I don't know why but I just followed the signs that said 'Chapel'. I kept saying to myself inside my head, I won't go in if there's someone already in there. But when I peeped through the glass door the chapel was empty. I was drawn inside by the silence. My eyes scanned the space... no chaplain, good... he often visits wards in the afternoon. Today I could talk to God on my own. Then I saw the candles; the sign said...

Candles 10p

I decided to light two candles (one for me and one for James) and promised God that I would bring the money another time. I would pay God on Sunday when Dad gave me my pocket money. I felt God would understand. Then, in the solemn surroundings, I suddenly did something that I have never done in my life before. I sank down to my knees, closed my eyes and I prayed. At the end of my prayer I said 'Please God make us both better.' Then, I looked at the wide aisle and imagined what it would be like if James and I got married. I walked up to the entrance door and imagined that my dad was walking me down the aisle. Then, when I got to the altar I pretended that James and I were exchanging vows. 'Gwendoline Ann Evans... will you take this man, James Michael Harrington to be your lawful, wedded husband?'

'I do. I do. I doooooooo!' I shouted out loudly.

Unfortunately, just at that exact moment the chaplain returned. He must have entered by another door. I apologised profusely but he just laughed and said,

'Don't forget if you want to have a chat... I am always around. I can arrange weddings too.'

He even picked up a newspaper article from a table at the back and said,

'This is a photo of the last wedding in our hospital chapel.'

I was so embarrassed... trust me to get caught!

cHAPTER tWENTY-tHREE - fAB 208 pARTY

sWANSEA (1974)

'You're a star Gwenny,' said Mum, 'you've been to the newsagents and bought the *Evening Post* for us.'

'Only because I wanted to find out what pop stars will be at the *FAB 208* party on Saturday,' replied Gwenny.

'Who are you going with?'

'Remember, my friend, Susan from youth club? Her parents said they would take us to Swansea in their car.'

'That's kind of them. Will you need some money for something to eat?'

'I think we're having lunch at Susan's house before we go.'

'What are you wearing? Poncho, denim jeans and sneakers?'

'Oh no, Mum they're for kids. Susan said I can borrow a pair of her new hot pants…and I'm going to wear my long, maxi cardigan and my navy patent shoes.'

'You'll look a right mess as usual,' scoffed Beth coming into the room and slamming the door behind her.

'Beth, I've told you umpteen times, don't slam that door.'

'It wasn't me Mum. It was the wind.'

Then Beth turned to Gwenny. 'What are you going to do with your hair?'

'My hair is okay… isn't it Mum? I'm going to wash it with *Silvikrin* shampoo to make it shine. Mum, am I allowed to wear make-up?'

'Yeah… if you want to look like a clown,' Beth interrupted.

'Sorry Gwenny,' continued Mum, 'I know you want to look grown up but you're only thirteen and you know what your dad is like. There would be ructions if he saw you wearing make-up. I would never hear the end of it.'

'Why don't you buy some make-up and put it on at Susan's,' Rosie whispered to Gwenny, 'Dad will never know.'

'Thanks Rosie, I'll do that.'

'Oh Gwenny, you're so lucky. I wish I was coming with you.'

'Sorry Rosie but you have to be a *FAB 208* club member. We sent away for the tickets. Susan got them ages ago. Oooh Rosie I'm so excited… I might even meet some famous pop stars.'

Gwenny and Susan joined the line of teenagers at the hotel entrance of the Dolphin hotel. A small group of parents were hovering around as the teenagers queued in front of the entrance sign *FAB 208* party. Gwenny had never been in such a long queue in her life.

'We're going to be here for hours,' she moaned, as she realised that the new navy shoes were pinching her toes and the trendy patterned tights kept wrinkling at the ankles.

Gwenny couldn't help noticing that other girls in the line were sniggering and pointing at them both.

'I wish I was wearing my denim jeans and sneakers,' Gwenny whispered to Susan.

'Don't look at them,' warned Susan, 'they're only jealous. These hot pants are fab. Even Pan's People were wearing them on *Top of the Pops.*'

'We're going around the shops now,' said Susan's father, returning to the queue, 'but we'll pick you up at six o'clock. The doorman says you'll be out by then.'

'Thanks for the lift Mr and Mrs Watkins,' said Gwenny quickly, remembering her manners.

'It's a pleasure. Remember to behave yourselves but have a good time.'

'We will,' they chorused in unison.

Inside the hotel, the girls were ushered to a conference room for the *FAB 208* party. The tables and chairs were arranged around the side of the big room but not many teenagers were bothered about sitting down. Gwenny and Susan joined the throng in the centre of the room where *FAB* representatives were giving out free goodie bags.

'Bags I… the mascara,' called one girl to her friend.

'Don't you get one each?' asked Susan, to a girl in front of them.

'Looks like you may have to share as each bag has different items.'

'That's not fair,' said Susan, 'but at least we can share easily because we see each other in school every day.'

'It's okay, you don't have to share,' replied Gwenny, 'my dad won't let me wear make-up. I'll have to wash it off today before I go home. I wish I had your parents Susan, they let you do what you like.'

'Yeah, I suppose they do. But I'd rather be in your family Gwenny; you have two sisters and a brother for company. I often get home from school and have to be on my own until one of my parents come home from work.'

'I would love the peace and quiet,' replied Gwenny, thinking of how noisy her home was.

'We'll have to swap houses one night,' Susan joked.

Just then they spotted a couple of vacant chairs so they sat down and emptied out the bags of free goodies.

'Do you want the nail polish or the eye shadow?'

'Don't mind,' said Gwenny, 'I won't be able to use either with my dad's beady eyes.'

'What about the lip salve? He can't stop you using that… it's colourless.'

'Okay, I'll have that.'

'Look, here's a free copy of *FAB 208*, you can have this one because I've already bought this week's magazine.'

'Did your father let you put the poster up on your bedroom wall?'

'Of course he did. He never stops me doing anything.'

'You're so lucky. My dad gets really mad if we don't listen to him.'

Just then a voice announced that the band would start to play in ten minutes.

'Quick Gwenny, let's shove the make-up in our handbags. We have to get to the front of the stage.'

Susan led the way across the dance floor and entered the throng of teenagers already milling to the front of the stage.

'My friend is claustrophobic so we have to be near the front,' Susan lied so that they could pass through the crowd. They ended up right next to the stage. A group of four boys were already setting up their musical instruments.

'This is going to be fun,' exclaimed Susan, as she smiled and fluttered her false eyelashes at the lead singer.

'Stop it…it, Susan,' stuttered Gwenny as she noticed how all the boys in the group kept staring at their hot pants

When the group had played several songs, the lead singer walked over to the front of the stage. He leaned over the small barriers and whispered something in Susan's ear.

'I'm going to meet him in his dressing room after the gig,' announced Susan proudly.

'What about your mum and dad?'

'They'll be fine. They're used to waiting around for me.'

Gwenny however, was not used to waiting around for Susan, and after ten minutes of standing on her own she decided to find the dressing room. She asked the security guard and followed his instructions. No one was around in the basement rooms as she knocked on the door. After a few minutes the door opened, and Gwenny saw Susan and the lead singer kissing on the sofa in the corner. She started to close the door when a low voice called her back.

'Hey Goldilocks,' grunted the lead guitarist as he tried to grab her arm but she quickly pulled away and slammed the door.

Oh God thought Gwenny, as she ran down the corridor *I wish I wasn't such a scared baby. I wish I was older like Susan. I wish I was brave enough to kiss a boy!*

A few minutes later Susan reappeared in the conference room where the party was being held.

'I've got a date with Maurice. He's the lead singer.'

'I saw you kissing him in the dressing room.' stated Gwenny.

'Were you spying on me?'

'No. I did knock but the guitarist tried to grab my arm and I got scared. I'd love to flirt with the boys like you do Susan but I'm a bit of a scared baby.'

'Nonsense,' said Susan. 'I had my first boyfriend when I was your age. But Maurice is different. He's two years older than me. He's going to phone me next weekend and we're going on a date. Oh… Gwenny, I think I'm falling in love at sixteen. Oooh… it's just like that film called *Love Story*.'

'But Susan… he had his hand up your jumper and you weren't stopping him.'

'Oh Gwenny… it was only a bit of fun.'

'But Susan. All the boys in the group were wearing make-up and eyeliner!'

'Yeah and why not? All the young people in Carnaby Street in London are wearing flowers in their hair.'

'I think I'm glad I live in Wales.'

'You're so old fashioned Gwenny. You need to be a bit trendier. We're the children of the future; not the past.'

By this time, the party was over everyone had left the party venue and so they made their way to the front lobby to meet up with Susan's parents.

'There's my mum and dad,' exclaimed Susan. 'Remember Gwenny, don't mention Maurice. Not even my parents are that broad-minded!'

The car drew up outside the main entrance. A few minutes later, Susan was excitedly telling her parents all about the party. She was careful to leave out the details of making a date with the lead singer. Gwenny sighed and found that all the excitement had been too much. She put her head on the back of the seat and closed her eyes.

'Sorry but I can't stay awake……..' she muttered to herself.

Gwenny was fast asleep before the car drove out of Swansea.

cHAPTER tWENTY-fOUR – 'uP oN tHE rOOF'

cHILDREN'S cANCER wARD, sOUTHAMPTON (1976)

'Gwenny, are you awake? It's time to go and find a shooting star,' whispered James as he quietly entered her hospital room.

'I'm ready,' murmured Gwenny. She jumped out of bed. She was already dressed in her warm jogging suit.

'I'll wait for you at the fire exit door,' said James, trying to hide his excitement. 'Don't be long…the moon and the stars are waiting.'

Gwenny checked the outside corridor to make sure that no one was around. Then she quietly closed the door. She could hear the sound of voices as she rearranged her pillows and popped them under the sheets. Next, she tucked the bed cover around the pillows just in case someone checked on her. Then, Gwenny put on her plimsolls. She did the laces up tightly and checked her appearance in the mirror.

'Oh, Gwenny,' she whispered to herself. 'You look so pale.'

She quickly searched her pocket for a lip shiner and put some colour on her lips.

'Much better,' she nodded at herself in the mirror.

A few minutes later, Gwenny met James by the fire exit door. He pointed at the stairs and instantly her face changed to dismay. She shook her head.

'I don't think I can climb all those stairs,' she said, doubtfully looking at James.

'Of course you can, Gwenny Evans. Where's your sense of adventure?' admonished James.

He paused and waited. 'Look, we've managed to escape from

the ward. This may be our only chance to get up to the roof to see the stars. It's got to be tonight because it's a clear night and it's a full moon… and… it's perfect.'

Gwenny shook her head but James continued to encourage her.

'Come on Gwenny Evans… you can do it. You've only been stuck in the isolation for six weeks. It could have been worse … you could still be there.'

Gwenny smiled at his words. 'James how come..?' she started.

'Oh, do be quiet Gwenny Evans and let's climb the stairs. You don't want the night security guard to catch us…do you?'

'Thought you said he'd be on his tea break.'

'He is…but he'll be back soon. So move lazy girl.'

'Me…lazy? I'll show you… you… you imbecile!'

James laughed. His face took on a whole new appearance when he was animated.

'Come on, Gwenny Evans, you've been shut up like a prisoner far too long.'

She took hold of the stainless steel handrail that ran alongside the stairs and moved slowly up onto the first step. Inside her head she just kept repeating the words *I can do this.* She used her hands to help lift her stiff legs and stepped up onto the second step. Her knees clicked with the unaccustomed action but as she dragged the other foot forward it began to be easier. She felt a bit wobbly but was reassured with James by her side.

'There… that's it, Gwenny Evans. You're doing well. You're amazing. You're my perfect little girlie. So brave…So strong… So determined.'

He continued to encourage her as he overtook her on the stairs

'Sh! Sh!...I can do it,' as he tried to help her once more. 'I'm alright on my own.'

'Okay, I'll leave you alone,' responded James, taking his hands away.

'See, no hands,' he teased, as he gambolled up the stairs. He was making monkey sounds and acting like an ape.

A few minutes later, a breathless but triumphant Gwenny reached the top step. James was already sitting grinning at the top of the stairs.

'What kept you?' he asked, pointing to his watch.

'I did it,' Gwenny gasped, as she took a deep breath. 'I did it, and it'll be a lot easier going down.'

'That's my girlie.'

'I'm not your girlie tonight. You didn't say that I would have to climb a thousand steps to get onto the roof. I thought there would be a lift at least.'

'Gwenny... you climbed one flight of stairs!'

'Okay. So what's next?'

'No more stairs,' he promised and pointed to the green fire exit doors in front of them.

'They're probably alarmed,' Gwenny warned.

'That's exactly what I thought,' agreed James. 'I actually tried them out earlier on today.'

'One... two... three,'

They pushed together. The bar lowered and both doors fell open. A stream of hot air nearly swept Gwenny's hat away and the strong, clinical smell of the hospital blasted in her face.

'Its okay, it's only the fan from the air conditioning unit behind this door.'

They carefully ventured out further onto the flat hospital roof.

'Wow... its so cold.' shivered Gwenny, hating the chill of the night air.

'Come here. I'll wrap my arms around you... then you won't be so cold.'

'Ooooh that's better. Look at the lights James. They're everywhere!'

'Come here.'

He led her to a spot where they had a clear view down to the docks and over to the oil refinery in the distance.

'So...Gwenny Evans. What do you think of this view? I promised I would give you the moon and the stars. Look how clear the sky is.'

They stood looking for a few moments mesmerized by the hundreds of twinkling stars in the sky.

'You said it was a full moon but half of it is missing.'

'It's behind the clouds, Dumbo.'

'Where's the north star James?' she asked. 'You said you would point it out.'

'I believe that's the north star,' he answered pointing up. 'Can you see the formation of stars? There Gwenny Evans over there. See four corners and then a couple of stars go out to the side. It's called the plough; it's a constellation of stars.'

'Oh... what about that twinkling star over there?'

'Gwenny Evans... that's not a star... that's moving. It's a plane just about to land at Southampton Airport.'

'Oops...silly me! But James... you promised me a shooting star.'

'You have to be very lucky to see one,' admitted James. But listen, Gwenny E\vans, if you could have any star in the universe which one would you choose? Go on, you pick and I'll try and catch it for you.'

'Catch a falling star and put it in your pocket save it for a rainy day,' hummed Gwenny as she obediently searched for her favourite star.

'Some stars are much brighter than others. I think I'll have that one?'

Gwenny pointed to the right.

'Close your eyes Gwenny Evans and no peeping. Let's see if I can catch it for you…yeah…oops…watch out. I just caught it.'

With that he produced a tiny shiny, silver foil star from the pocket of his fleecy jacket.

'I told you that I'd give you the moon and the stars. So there's the full moon and here is your own little star to treasure forever. I hope it will make all your wishes come true'

He kissed the star, opened her fingers and placed it in the palm of her hand.

'Oh…James!'

'Gwenny Evans… I love you more than the stars and the moon and the sun and… and….'

He planted a kiss lightly on her lips.

'But you're my favourite star…Gwenny Evans. I don't know how I would have got through the last few weeks if it hadn't been for you.'

'I love you too James, since the first time I saw you.'

Gwenny smiled, thinking *I will never ever, ever… forget this moment. The moment that James told me he loved me under the stars. It will stay with me forever and ever and ever and ever.* She shivered in delight.

'I can see you're cold. We'd best go back inside.'

They walked arm in arm to the doors. James let go of her hand to open the doors but the bar would not budge. James tried again but the doors remained shut. He then put his shoulder to both doors and pushed with all his strength.

'Come on James. Stop teasing me.'

'Gwenny Evans, I am not teasing,' James insisted, 'The door won't open.'

'I thought you said you'd tried it yesterday.'

'I did but then I was on the other side. I didn't try it from this side. The breeze must have blown it shut.'

'Here let me. I bet I can open it,' Gwenny suggested. She held the bar tightly, pressing down with all her might. The doors remained shut.

'Oh God… we're trapped.'

There was silence as neither of them dared utter a word. After a few seconds Gwenny broke the silence

'James… please say something, I'm getting cold out here. I'll end up having to go back in isolation at this rate.'

He replied slowly, as reality hit.

'Gwenny Evans, I don't think there's another way down.'

'Don't be silly. There has to be.'

'Well, I came up here the other day and I could only find this exit. The rest of the hospital has different levels of roof space.'

'But James, there wouldn't only be one way onto the roof.'

'Well… I couldn't find another exit to the roof from this floor.'

'Oh, God,' Gwenny shivered, 'what are we going to do?'

'I don't know. Perhaps someone will realise we're missing and they'll search up here.'

'But why would they think of checking the roof?'

'I don't know.'

'Oh… James. I'm so sorry. It's my fault. I was the one who asked you to give me the stars and the moon. Now we're both going to be ill again because of me.'

'If I can fight my cancer I'm sure I can find a way down from this roof,' stated James, suddenly feeling determined. He stood up straight and tall, pushing back his shoulders. 'There must be another exit and I'm going to find it.'

Just then the moon came out from behind a cloud and James spotted a ladder that descended to a lower part of the hospital roof.'

'Ok… what are you like on ladders?'

'Ladders… no problem,' reassured Gwenny.

'I'll go first,' suggested James. 'You wait here, in case it's a dead end.'

'Oooh James, I'm not staying here by myself.'

'Who's going to get you? Do you think the man the in the moon is going to grab you? There's no one else up here.'

'Okay then… but be quick.'

'I'll be back in a jiffy.'

Several minutes later, James climbed back up the ladder.

'No way out… Gwenny Evans. We'll just have to spend the rest of the night up here on the roof. The warmest part is behind the doors, where the fans are blowing warm air, so we won't freeze.'

Minutes later, they cuddled together on James's fleecy jacket, warm and snug by the air vent.

'James, can you say goodnight to everyone in the world?'

'Gwenny, are you delirious?'

'No, I am just remembering the times during my childhood when I couldn't go to sleep. Clemmie would come and sit by my bed and he would say good night to everyone in the world. He'd speak in a whisper because we didn't want to wake anyone up. He'd say… *Let's say good night to Mummy. Goodnight to Daddy. Goodnight to Beth and Rosie.* Then, he'd look around my bedroom and say good night to all my toys, first the panda, then the teddy and then the dolls. After that he'd say good night to all the animals in the zoo… the lions, the tigers, the giraffes and he'd tell the elephants to stop swinging their trunks because it was time to go to bed.

Finally, he'd say goodnight to all the animals on the farm. He'd say *Cows... stop eating your grass because it's time to go to bed.'*

'James, do you get the idea? You can be Clemmie and say goodnight to everyone. Are you still awake? James! James!'

There was no reply.

'James, you're asleep,' Gwenny giggled, shaking him gently.

'What? I must have dozed off,'

'I sent you to sleep,' Gwenny laughed and snuggled into his body. 'James… I love you.'

He pretended to snore gently this time.

'James, you can't be asleep. You haven't said goodnight to the printing press.'

'I'll say goodnight for you,' interrupted a gruff male voice as they felt the door behind them being moved. They both jumped up. It was the night security guard.

'I thought I heard voices. What on earth are you two doing up here?'

'Sorry,' apologised James, 'We just wanted to some fresh air and we got trapped here because the door blew shut.'

'I could get you two into lots of trouble,' said the security guard, 'but you haven't even been reported missing yet. If I was you two I would creep back into your ward. If you go now, I won't report you. But if I catch you two again… look out! It's a good job I had to check the fire extinguishers tonight or I wouldn't have found you….so scoot!'

They both mumbled *Thank you.* Then, holding hands, they slowly and stiffly descended the stairs.

'At least he let us off, 'whispered Gwenny. 'But how will we get back into the ward?'

James paused for a moment, then he answered, 'If you are challenged by a member of staff just say that you needed drink from the machine down the corridor and I'll …I'll think of something. I'll say that I must have been sleep walking! It's my new chemo. It makes me sleep walk, I just made up a brand new side effect.'

James giggled. Gwenny grinned.

'Oh Gwenny Evans…I am so sorry, it's all gone wrong but...we did have fun… didn't we?'

He hugged her quickly, grinning in the dimmed corridor light.

'Psst… James. You didn't say goodnight to the printing press.'

Gwenny poked out her tongue and opened the ward door. She could hear the rattle of bed pans in the sluice room. Good, the nurses were still busy. Gwenny crept into her room. She didn't need a light. She knew every inch of this room like the back of her hand. She took her journal out of her drawer. She opened the lock with the key, switched on her torch and started to write in the torchlight. The words seemed to dance across the page.

Thursday, March 11 (10.00.p.m.)

Let me be the star in James's life.

Like an everlasting twinkling star

Shining radiantly as I enter the pathways of life.

Let me be more than just a tiny speck,

May I be strong with a sense of purpose.

Let me be the shooting star in James's life.

Goodnight dear dairy. I know I am in love for the very first time. He loves me, he loves me not, he loves mmeeeeeeeeeeeeeeeeeeeeeeeeeeeeeeee!!!!!!!!!!!!!!!!!!!!!!!!

cHAPTER tWENTY-fIVE - mOVING aND bULLYING

wALES/eNGLAND (1975)

Mum and Dad were trying to explain to their daughter why the family were uprooting and moving from Wales to Hampshire.

'Gwenny, listen, Dad isn't doing this just for himself. He's doing it because he loves us. He wants us to have a nice house and enough money for us to send you to university. Please explain again Moc, so that Gwenny can understand why we have to move,' pleaded Mum.

'Well firstly,' Dad begun, 'I am leaving the colliery because my eyesight problems mean I can no longer work down in the mine. I'll have a small payoff, not much, but together with the money from the sale of our house and the printing press I'll be able to buy my own printing business in Southampton. It's an established business, not like my old printing shed in the garden. So instead of *Miskin Press*, I will be the owner of *Miskin Printers*. There'll be no more shift work, no more working on the coal face and I'll be my own boss.'

'Will you be able to print my poems, Dad?'

'Yes, but much more quickly because the new printing press is more modern and efficient.'

'But… what about Clemmie?'

'He has promised to come to stay every school holiday and at special times Christmas and Easter and…and…whenever we need him.'

'Dad, I don't want to move. What about my school and Beth's university?'

'You will study for your GCSE 'O' levels in the local secondary modern school and Beth will go to university in Southampton.'

'Aren't there any grammar schools in Southampton?'

'You'll need to pass an entrance examination so until you do, you'll go to the secondary modern school near our new house. Now don't make a fuss and don't spoil it for the rest of us. It's going to be the making of our family. This is an opportunity not to be missed.'

Gwenny shook her head and began to mutter *It's not fair…* but Dad interrupted.

'Let's not hear any more moans and groans Gwenny. Our family is moving to Hampshire… and you, young lady…you are coming with us.'

The move went well and before Gwenny knew it, she was a few weeks into the Autumn term. Unfortunately, she did not settle well into her new school. She felt ill every day. Everyone said she was suffering from homesickness. But most days Gwenny's head throbbed, her eyes felt heavy and she experienced unbearable tiredness. She couldn't understand why, but she just knew that she had to lie down and that's how she came to be hiding in the P.E. shed at lunchtime. She was just curling up on the soft mattress in her woollen duffle coat when she was aroused by noisy laughter coming from outside the shed. She tiptoed across the floor and crouched down behind the door. The first words she heard were in a mimicking tone. Gwenny recognised the unmistakable sound of a distinctive loud voice. It was Daisy Bishop and her cronies.

'She's got a new satchel… a real leather one. She said it was her sister's but then I spotted her name written in black ink on the inside flap. So then she said that her uncle bought it for her. What a lie! Uncles don't buy real leather satchels. She said he got it for her because she was moving from Wales.'

'He was probably glad to get rid of her,' laughed Tania, the one they all called Shuff.

'Stuck up little madam,' Daisy chipped in. 'Did you see the coat she was wearing today? A duffle coat! They are so old-fashioned nowadays. No one wears duffle coats anymore!'

The group laughed loudly. Daisy, encouraged by their response, continued to speak.

'Yeah… what about her sensible school shoes? They're lace-ups, not even a little heel. How old does she think she is? Five?'

'Listen to this. Linda found spare uniform in her gym bag. Why does she bring a change of clothes to school…is it in case she wets herself?'

The group sniggered.

'How did you find her spare clothes Linda?' asked Shuff.

'I had to check her bag last week when I lost my white socks. So I asked her why she had spare clothes and she said in case she falls over. She does trip up a lot; that's why she has so many bruises. But hang on a minute, why do you all hate her so much?'

Daisy answered immediately.

'Because she's got everything we haven't got. She's pretty. She's got thick, wavy hair which she doesn't even have to dye. She's clever… and…and…' She paused a moment trying to think of other reasons. Finally, she added,

'She's got a *Parker* fountain pen.'

'How do you know she has a *Parker* fountain pen?'

'I'm looking after it for her. It's in my pocket safe and sound.' Daisy patted the inside pocket of her school blazer. 'She's always losing her things. Haven't you noticed, Linda?'

'But Daisy, you can't hate someone because she's got a leather satchel and a *Parker* pen?'

'She shouldn't try and get things better than us then. Her family even have two cars!'

'You seem to know a lot about someone that you dislike immensely, but how do you know all these things?'

'Well, my sister, Sandra was doing her paper round over on the new estate when she spotted Gwenny getting out of a car driven by her mother.'

'That's because her mother's a teacher.'

'Yeah, why is her mother a teacher? Our mums just work as school cleaners or in the shops in town.'

'She's a teacher so that they can afford the new house. She told me they need the five bedrooms when their family come to stay.'

'What family does she mean…the Welsh nut cases that visit them from the *Land of the Red Dragon*?'

'Do you think you are being fair to her?' asked a new voice, a much kinder voice.

'Fair. What does fair mean? Is life fair? She gets more Grade 'A's than the rest of us put together.' Daisy almost spat her words.

'But she can't help being intelligent.'

'She's a bloody little swot.'

'You're only jealous, Daisy, because you used to be top of the class before she came.'

'So...she should have thought of that before she came here. She should have had Grade 'B's... then, we'd still like her.'

'But how is she supposed to know that? She actually seems quite nice if you talk to her.'

'Oh shut up... you sound as if you are sticking up for her,' scoffed Daisy.

'So you've taken her pen?' Linda chipped in.

'Yep...plus her bus pass. I hid it somewhere where she won't ever find it.'

'No... don't tell me. It's in the school incinerator... isn't it?'

'Where else would I keep it safe?' laughed Daisy. 'We've got to make sure that she doesn't come back here next term.'

'And how will you do that?' Linda asked.

'We're just going to 'lose' all her things. We'll try and get that little key she wears around her neck when she takes it off for hockey lessons. Then, we'll hide her sandwiches and her dinner money. And we'll put the blame on the new first formers...they're always in lots of trouble.'

'So what do you plan to do first?'

'Let's make sure we get one of those books she's always scribbling poems in. They're her prize possessions. Even Miss Pudson made comments about how good her poems are.'

'And then?'

'Then... we'll start writing the anonymous notes!'

cHAPTER tWENTY-sIX – bRUISES

cHILDREN'S cANCER wARD, sOUTHAMPTON (1976)

Sunday, March 14 (11.00 a.m.)

One of the nurses just brought me a note.

Mum going to be late this evening. Trouble with car. She will see you about 8 p.m.

This is my last night in hospital so I can put up with Mum being a little late.

Monday, March 15 (9.00 p.m.)

I'm home. I simply can't believe it. I've had such a fun time with my family again. Everyone's been so lovely. Even Beth came home from university to welcome me home. What an honour! I wish I could have come home earlier today but I had to wait around for my medication, then the needles, then the saline and then the yellow bucket to put the old needles in. There is so much baggage that comes with me these days! I just can't pack a bag anymore: I have to pack one bag just for my medical needs. My welcome home tea party was great; lots of little presents and even a cake. But now I have managed to escape to my own little bedroom. I'm so tired I could sleep for a week. I didn't realise how much I had missed home. I keep noticing little things about my room that I hadn't even seen before. It's like I'm seeing it all again with new eyes. I simply can't take in that everything is exactly as I left it all those weeks ago. I find it hard to believe that Rosie and Gareth haven't even messed up my things. My bookcase is still neatly stacked with all my books in alphabetical order. No one has even moved my beer mat collection. They're still displayed around the room. I'm always collecting something and this year I'm collecting beer mats. The adults in my family are always saving them for me. On my wall by the door are my captions for the week. They're a bit out of date now. I haven't been home for over six weeks. I love quotes and I am always searching for a new one to write on my lovely Betsey Clarke memo pad. Sometimes I choose words from books or magazines or other times, lines from songs I hear on the radio. I love having words in my life. I read the last three quotes that I had written before I went into hospital.

Love is the reward of love.

Caring ways make lovely days.

Happy memories are to treasure.

I love being here back in my own little bedroom with the glow from my special green lava lamp. All of a sudden I feel a rush of emotions and I find tears are falling onto the pages of my diary. Why am I crying when I am supposed to be so happy? The day after tomorrow is the book launch. I am so excited. I don't think I'll ever go to sleep. I notice Dad has put my little black and white portable television in my room. It looks out of place perched on the end of my dressing table. I'll need a new little table so that I can watch television in bed. My room has such a lovely, homely smell as I realise Mum has hung some lavender sachets near my bedside table. I can hear the hum of the central heating and the creak of the floorboards as our house almost basks in the warmth of our central heating. There's a smell of clean, fresh bed linen and I lift the top sheet to my nose. Home!

My own little bed
My pillow is perfect for me
Soft and feathery,

Smooth and comforting.

My sheets are perfect for me

Clean and fresh,

Silky and caressing.

My duvet is perfect for me

Warm and welcoming,

Squishy and squashy

My bed is perfect for me,

Firm and familiar,

Cosy and comforting

My family is perfect for me

Lovely and loving

Cuddles and 'cwtches'

This is where I finally feel safe and secure,

Happy and content

I am home… home at last!

Tuesday, March 15 (7.00 a.m.)

I still can't believe I came home yesterday and after all the excitement I am lying here cuddling my cosy old blankets and listening to the familiar sounds of home. I can't understand why I'm finding it so quiet. Then I realise there are no monitors going beep, no bed alarms, no constant movements. Home… peace at last!

I can tell that it's bin day without looking out of the window; the rubbish van screeches as it reverses into our cul-de-sac. I can hear the crash of metal as bins are emptied onto the big truck. I can hear the men's voices as they shout to each other.

7.30 a.m. - The bin men have gone now and I concentrate on listening to voices from downstairs. Gareth's and Rosie's voices are the ones that I can easily pick out. They're always bickering and quarrelling. Even the air is different at home instead of the stifling heat of the hospital. The central heating at home has a friendly hum and I can put my toes on the radiators without burning the soles of my feet. I can smell Mum's cooking...she's frying bacon for Dad's breakfast. He always has egg and bacon for breakfast on Tuesdays because Mum doesn't have to be in so early. It's reassuring that some things never change!

8.00 a.m. - Mum just brought a bacon sandwich and a nice cup of tea to my bedroom. She says it's my homecoming treat and I mustn't expect it again. She reminded me that James is coming to my house today. Dad is bringing TWO hundred copies of my book home this afternoon, for me and James to sign. I don't think I've ever been so excited in all my life. It's as if my poems are being brought to life.

Hours later.

'It's my book launch tomorrow James. I'm so excited... I'm even going to be wearing my own hair. Not a wig!'

James smiled, 'Gwenny Evans tries out a new cropped hairstyle instead of bald.'

'Stop teasing me James.'

Gwenny looked into the mirror. Her hair was growing back. It was still very short for a girl, but at least she had hair. No more itchy wigs... what a relief!

'I'm surprised at how beautiful I look... even if I say so myself,' mimicked James, as he stood behind her as she looked in the mirror.

Gwenny looked at James and they both burst out laughing. He ruffled her tufty hair.

'You look gorgeous my little Gwenny Evans… everyone will envy your beautiful but very short, wavy hair.'

A few minutes later, Gwenny ran upstairs and changed into her new outfit for the book launch. Mum had ordered from the catalogue. The skirt and blouse fitted her perfectly. James picked up a newspaper lying on the table rolled it up into a tube and pretended it was a microphone.

'Here we have our newest cat walk model; Miss Gwenny Evans. Today she is wearing a cream cheesecloth blouse and a blue patterned Indian skirt to match her eyes.'

'I absolutely love it,' sighed Gwenny. 'It's been so long since I had any new clothes. I'm so thrilled. Ahhhhhhhhhhhhhhhhhh!'

'Well, it certainly beats the pyjamas and dressing gown look,' commented James. 'So now we've had your fashion show…what's next?'

'I'll just go and change back into my jogging outfit and then we'll get on with signing the books.' said Gwenny as she tiptoed across the room being careful not to fall in her long skirt.

Minutes later they sat by the dining room table side by side writing their signatures.

'Are you sure that the illustrator signs the books too?'

'Well, not really… but you've done such a good job. I just want people to know that the illustrations are all yours.'

They continued to work in silence for a few minutes while Gwenny flipped through one of the books for the hundredth time.

'The book's perfect but I'm not deluded. It would never have been printed if it hadn't been for your help.

'I know a lot of people like reading poetry but your illustrations bring my poems alive. What would I have done without you?'

'It was Jackie's idea not mine. If your father didn't own his printing business we could have found it difficult for anyone to print the books,' reminded James.

'Yeah, but Jackie and Dad couldn't have done the illustrations. I don't know which drawing I like best. I love your snowflake design on the black coloured page. I love your interpretation of *'Rain.'* But I think my overall favourite is '*The Printing Press'* drawing. Oh James, when did you get to be so talented?'

'I've always loved drawing… but your poems! They inspired me to draw again Gwenny Evans. I just didn't have the motivation because I was feeling ill. The good thing is that we're going to raise so much money by selling this book for the ward. You and me… we're a team.'

'James. Can I tell you something? You must promise me that you won't tell anyone else.'

James nodded.

'My legs are covered in bruises. Do you think I should tell Dr Neville?'

'Yes, I think you should. You know they told us to look out for unusual signs… like a rash or bruises. It may mean you are having a slight reaction to your treatment…let me see.'

He glanced down as she pulled up her jogging bottoms to reveal her legs.

'Nice pins…Gwenny Evans.' James teased. Then, he saw the bruises, 'Oh, my God. You'd better mention it to Dr Neville…but perhaps it would be better after the book launch.'

cHAPTER tWENTY-sEvEN – sIGNS
sOUTHAMPTON (1975)

I have started keeping a diary. Clemmie bought it for me to encourage me to write every day. He wants me to record not only where I go or what I do. He says I need to write about my feelings. He is convinced that this type of writing will encourage me to write poems. He even managed to find one with a tiny lock so that it can be kept private. I am going to wear the key on a little silver chain around my neck so it will never go missing.

There are ten bruises on my legs today. Why do I have bruises in England? I didn't have bruises in Wales. I miss Wales so much. I miss seeing Clemmie every day. I miss Susan and I miss my old school. In fact, I miss everything about Wales, even the way people talk. It's so different living in England; whenever I open my mouth someone comments about my accent. No one ever seems to understand what I am saying. Everyone seems to think I am stupid. I constantly get asked to repeat things and so I have to speak extra slowly. It's so embarrassing.

Clemmie told me to write down all of my worries and concerns. Well, here's one…I keep on having nosebleeds. I think I've had one every day this week. Mum has started asking who's using all the tissues and so I've had to pinch lots of toilet paper from the bathroom cupboard. I use it to stuff up my nose. I've gone through two rolls already… it takes ages for the nosebleeds to stop. I hope I don't get one in school. I've put spare clothes in my gym kit just in case.

<u>*Friday*</u>

Yesterday I heard Daisy and the rest of the bullies talking outside the P.E. shed. Now I know who's doing all the nasty things to me. I'll make sure that I lock my books and satchel in my locker and then they won't be able to get any of my stuff. I know I should tell someone but I have no proof and who will believe me? The bullies will only deny it. I'm just the new girl around here and so the teachers will think I'm making it up. It's not even worth trying! I don't want to go to school anymore. It's making me so unhappy; if only Clemmie was here he would know what to do. I can't tell Mum. She is too busy with her new teaching job and Dad is working all hours in his printing business. So there's simply no one else. I'll just have to hope that the bullies will get fed up and pick on someone else. I've counted the bruises on my legs. There are now fourteen so I am wearing my tights under my long socks but I absolutely dread P.E. lessons. I've written a note on behalf of my mum, it took me ages as I had to disguise my writing.

Dear Miss Morris,

Please would you excuse Gwenny from taking part in P.E. today as she sprained her ankle yesterday afternoon.

Thank you,

Mrs J. Evans

'Gwenny. Gwenny… do you hear me? Get up or you are going to be late for school,' shouted Mum as she opened Gwenny's bedroom door and pulled back the curtains.

'But Mum… I'm so tired. I don't think I can go to school today.'

'What's up?' asked Mum, suddenly stopping by the bed.

'I couldn't sleep last night. My stomach's all swollen and very uncomfortable and I'm just tired out.'

'You do look pale. I'll try and get a doctor's appointment tomorrow and perhaps ask him to do a blood test too. I'll let the school know when I drop Rosie off. Then, I'll phone Dad to look in on you this morning and I'll pop home in my lunch hour to make sure you are alright.'

'Oh Mum… don't fuss. I'll be fine. I'll stay in bed so you don't have to worry.'

'Shall I make you a hot water bottle? Do you need some aspirin?'

'No, Mum. I'm just going to sleep it off. I'll be fine by tomorrow.'

'Okay… if you're sure.'

Then turning away she called out, 'Rosie…Gareth. Gwenny's not well today so she's not going to school.'

'That's not fair,' moaned Gareth. 'Last week when I wasn't well you still made me go to school.'

'That's because Mum knew you were pretending.' reminded Rosie. 'You just hadn't learnt your words for your spelling test.'

'Hush you two. Let Gwenny get some rest now.'

Minutes later Gwenny heard the car reversing out of the drive. She rose from her bed and padded across the landing into her parents' bedroom. She removed the medical dictionary from the bookshelves and looked up *bruising*. She read and re-read the words *'bruising usually occurs as a result of an injury but occasionally can be an indication of more serious diseases such as leukaemia or haemophilia'*.

'What are they?' she asked herself out loud. 'Surely I haven't got a serious illness? It's probably just a tummy bug.'

So placing the dictionary safely back on the shelf, she made her way back to her bedroom when the phone rang.

'Hello, Southampton 221785,' she waited for the pips to end as the person in a phone kiosk put in the coins. Then, she heard Clemmie's voice.

'Hello Gwenny, it's me. It's Clemmie. Mum phoned me and told me you're not feeling well. How are you cariad?'

His voice was full of love and concern. There was a long pause as she tried to stop her tears.

'Hello… Hello… Gwenny! Gwenny! What's the matter?'

She took a deep breath and blurted out. 'Oh… Clemmie, I'm so scared. I'm not feeling well and don't tell Mum but I keep having nosebleeds…(sniff, sniff) and I've fourteen bruises on my legs and I'm so tired all the time and my stomach's bad …and…and… please don't tell Mum. But I just got her medical dictionary off the shelf and it said… it said…(more sobbing). It said bruises mean leukaemia or haemophilia and I don't even now what they are.'

'Gwenny…listen. You must calm down. You're getting yourself into an awful state. You've probably got a tummy bug, or a virus. That will make your whole system out of sorts. The nosebleeds and bruises are because you are a bit run down.'

(More sobbing)

'But Gwenny, just in case... I'm getting the next train down to you.'

'You're what? You're coming today? Oh, Clemmie… you don't need to. I'll be better by tomorrow.'

'I'm coming today. Tell Mum when you see her lunchtime. I'll get a taxi from the station so I'll probably be there around 3 o'clock.'

'Thank you Clemmie. I love you soooo much,' said Gwenny, as she put down the phone and walked across the landing back to her own bedroom. Clemmie was coming; everything was going to be alright.

cHAPTER tWENTY-eIGHT – bOOK lAUNCH

sOUTHAMPTON (1976)

Gwenny was enjoying being home from hospital. Clemmie had come to stay for the book launch.

'Now calm down Gwenny,' warned Clemmie, entering the room. 'Or you are going to get ill again.'

'Don't worry, Clemmie. I'm fine.'

Unfortunately, later that day, Gwenny was not fine. Her Hickman line in her chest began to throb with a burning pain. She tried to mask how ill she felt but at bed time that night her temperature shot up. Mum had no choice but to call the hospital and ask for help. They advised Mum to check her temperature regularly during the next few hours. Mum was reassured and told Gwenny to calm down.

'You're far too excited about the book launch,' she said and advised Gwenny to rest. Half an hour later, Gwenny collapsed at the bottom of the stairs on the way to bed. It was time to tell the hospital they were on their way. Dad got the car out while Mum called Clemmie to come to the hospital with them. Then, they woke Beth to tell her what was happening. Meanwhile Mum grabbed the overnight bag which was already packed in case of an emergency.

Arriving at the hospital, they went straight to the children's cancer ward, where Doctor Neville assessed the situation and decided that Gwenny needed emergency surgery.

'But it's my book launch tomorrow morning!' wailed Gwenny, looking *like death*.

'Can you wait two days?' questioned Dad. 'As you know she's been working on a poetry book for a very long time and the book launch is arranged for tomorrow.'

'Mr and Mrs Evans,' said Doctor Neville, taking them both aside, 'I'll be completely honest with you. If we don't operate tonight, you may not have a daughter tomorrow.'

Mum begun to cry.

'Sorry doctor. We had no idea it was that serious,' said Dad, signing the consent form.

'Mum, don't leave me,' begged Gwenny.

'We have no choice darling,' consoled Mum, hugging Gwenny. 'You've got to have the operation tonight or you'll be very ill. You have an infection in your Hickman line. It has to be removed as soon as possible, or the infection will spread to other parts of your body.'

'Well, promise me one thing then,' moaned Gwenny, resigned to defeat. 'Please make sure that the book launch goes ahead. James and I have signed all the books and there're so many people coming.'

Gwenny's parents looked at each other, baffled as to what to say.

'I think we'd better cancel it,' suggested Dad.

'No, please don't do that,' screamed Gwenny. 'The children on the ward are waiting for the money for the portable syringes so that they won't have to stay in hospital so long. It's really important we get the money as soon as poss…'

Her words trailed off as the anaesthetic started to take effect and the theatre nurse indicated for Gwenny's parents to leave.

'Time to take her through to theatre,' whispered the nurse.

Gwenny was dozing, recovering from the previous night's operation when suddenly the door of her single bed ward burst open and Beth rushed into the room and flung herself onto the bed to hug Gwenny.

'Beth?' murmured Gwenny, groggily. 'What are you doing here?'

'Mum told me that you were seriously ill last night. I couldn't sleep a wink because I thought… I thought… you were dying. Don't die, Gwenny. I'm soooo sorry. I really am. Please say you'll forgive me. I was just being silly. And… uhh… I didn't mean to be so mean and nasty. It was me who stole your poem. I gave it to the other Gwenny Evans and she just changed some lines and gave it a different name and she won but it was your poem all along.'

'Beth… Beth…stop!' said Gwenny speaking more loudly. 'What are you saying? It was my poem after all. You stole my poem for the Eisteddfod all those years ago. I always wondered how the other Gwendoline Evans won. But Beth that was a long time ago so stop crying now…I forgive you… its ok… its ok. And about last night I was very poorly and of course, Mum had to tell you but I'm sorry she frightened you. You can see I'm alright now. They got the infected line out in time and after twelve hours of antibiotics and a blood transfusion I'm like a new person again. In fact, I feel better than I have felt for a long time. But of course I can't mix with a lot of people because my immune system needs at least twenty four hours to recover.'

'So… so… you're not going to die,' clarified Beth.

'Look at me Beth….do I look like someone who's dying?'

Beth shook her head.

'Listen, Beth. Dr Neville found an infection in my Hickman line and I had to have it taken out before all the bad germs spread into my body. They operated last night and I'm beginning to feel better already.'

'You're so brave, Gwenny.'

'No, Beth… you're brave too… you've had to put up with a heck of a lot. It can't have been easy with me having all the attention, all of the time!'

'Yeah… but… I was always a little bit jealous of you before you had cancer. I promise from now on I'll try….'

'Come here Beth,' said Gwenny, hugging her tightly, 'you don't have to make me any promises. No one's perfect but just do me one favour. I can't be there for the book launch today. So would you read one of my poems? You can read the one about the snow. You've always liked that.'

'Of course I will, Gwenny. I'm really sorry you can't attend your first book launch but there will be other times. I've got a feeling this won't be the last book you write.'

She began to walk towards the door but paused before she turned the handle.

'Gwenny, you're not the perfect sister either but I do love you. It's just that you're always so… serious, so… annoying. Do you know what? I'm going to carry on teasing you. And right now… I hate your hair. You look just like a boy!!'

With that Beth gave Gwenny a quick hug, stuck out her tongue and ran off down the corridor. Gwenny smiled as she heard Beth apologise as she nearly collided with the breakfast trolley.

That afternoon the hospital staff and all the dignitaries from the local cancer charity assembled in the hospital conference room. Some parents and children from the ward were there as Jackie announced,

'Good afternoon all and thank you for attending this book launch for our *Rainbows* poetry book, which we are selling today in aid of the Children's Cancer Ward. I just need to let you know that Gwenny Evans, the young lady, who wrote the poems for this book, was rushed into theatre last night with an infection. She is now recovering on the ward upstairs, but she has requested that we go ahead with the book launch. Gwenny's family are going to read some of her favourite poems. Then, James Harrington, who has illustrated the book, has agreed to talk through his favourite poems and show you the sketches he produced to illustrate the poems.'

During the next hour the poems were read and the audience clapped to show their appreciation. Gwenny's father made a fitting tribute. He apologised for Gwenny's absence, and invited all the audience to buy the book of poems.

'Sold out,' said Jackie, an hour later, counting up the money on the table in front of her. 'We've sold the books for £2.50 each and lots of people said keep the change. We've already raised well over £500.'

'Looks like we may have to print a second edition,' observed Dad.

'Gwenny will be over the moon,' commented Mum.

'She's done it, Moc,' said Clemmie, taking Dad aside, 'We've got our own little star of the future. She will go far. Just imagine how much determination it has taken to get this book completed when she's been fighting for her life.'

'It's your encouragement that has made her finally believe in herself. She's planning on going to university because she actually wants to study the poets that you have read to her. It's all down to your hard work Clemmie. I'm so proud of her.'

'Well Moc, I never thought I would hear you say that. You need to say those very words to Gwenny. She has spent her whole life trying to please you and make you proud of her. Remember when she was little how she used to long to help you in the printing shed. Well, she's still trying to gain your love and approval. Please tell her how you feel.'

'I will Clemmie. It seems I've been so caught up in the printing business that I haven't spent as much time as I would have liked with my family. I'm going to make it up to them all. Gwenny's brush with death has been a wake up call for me.'

Clemmie's eyes filled with tears.

'You are so right though Clemmie. I'll never know where she gets her guts and determination from.'

'She's got a bit of us all in her. You mark my words. That girl will go far. A new Welsh poet? Bard at the Eisteddfod? She's only fifteen years old. She has the world at her feet. Her work can only get better once she has studied for her degree. I will be so proud of her when she gets her cap and gown. My life's work will be done.'

'Don't say that Clemmie,' added Mum, joining the two men. 'You're beginning to sound as if you are saying goodbye.'

Mum brought Gwenny home from hospital at teatime the next day. Gwenny was overjoyed to be home again and listened while everyone related how well the book launch had gone. They had sold out of copies of the poetry book and Dad explained how he would have to do a reprint.

'This time I'll make sure I have enough. I'll print another two hundred copies,' claimed Dad.

With all the excitement Mum couldn't help but notice how quiet Clemmie was. He was smiling and joking with all the family, but Mum could see by his eyes that he wasn't his usual self.

'What's up Clemmie?' asked Mum.

'Sorry,' he said lowering his voice, 'I wanted to celebrate with you all but I have a few pains in my chest. I think it must be all the excitement. Don't worry…if I'm not better… I'll see the doctor tomorrow.'

'You won't get an appointment. Perhaps I should take you to accident and emergency department tonight.'

'Oh there's no need to bother. It's probably just a bit of indigestion.'

Mum watched his reaction and smiled gently.

'I'm fine,' he insisted, walking out of the room with Mum, 'I don't want to frighten the children'.

Just then another chest pain made Clemmie bend over. Sweat broke out on his brow. His pallor turned grey and his hands started to tremble.

'I'm ok, Jen,' he protested hoarsely, but he was far from well.

Clemmie collapsed in the car on the way to the hospital. Mum ran into A&E where they rushed him into intensive care.

Mum phoned Dad in a panic.

'Jen, he's in the best place. He'll be fine.' reassured Dad.

'I don't know what to think!' confessed Mum.

'Are you staying the night?'

'Yes, I'll stay with him.'

The next morning when Gwenny's mum returned from the hospital, she had a tear-stained face. She took one look at her children and sobbed out loud.

'He just died in my arms.'

Gwenny gasped in horror and Mum burst into floods of fresh tears. It set off a chain reaction because as soon as Rosie and Gareth saw Mum upset they started crying too. Gwenny stood helpless. It was then that Dad entered the room to see what was going on.

'Clemmie's gone,' stated Mum simply.

Dad walked across the room and hugged Mum. She sobbed in his arms.

'Enough.' Dad said looking first at Gwenny. 'Please take Rosie and Gareth upstairs Gwenny, they won't stop crying if they see Mum so upset.'

Gwenny hurried her younger siblings upstairs and then rushed into her own room. She buried her head in the winceyette pillowcase. The pillow had feathers: it was soft and welcoming like Clemmie's arms. But Clemmie was dead. There would be no arms to hold her safely anymore. She wouldn't see his kind, blue eyes again. She wouldn't be able to smell the familiar aroma of Woodbine when he held her in one of his big 'cwtches'. Who would read her poems? Who would buy her ice creams every day in the summer? Who would sing *Calon Lan* at the piano? All these thoughts raced through her head as her fist repeatedly hit the pillow. She punched it until she could punch no more.

Mum suggested that she read one of her poems at the funeral service, as Beth was doing the bible reading. Dad printed her poem on the order of service. She would read it at the graveside. She had written the poem when she was eleven years old.

Clemmie is love and security,

Safe feelings,

Fun and laughter,

Songs and rhymes,

He's a listener,

He's a problem solver,

He's my guardian angel

In a fluffy "cloud of perfectness".

I love him more then life itself.

He is such a big part of my family

I constantly feel his love.

It surrounds me. It protects me.

In my wonderful world of childhood.

Tears fell down her cheeks as she read the poem. Others cried too it was so obvious how Clemmie was much loved and respected by all. Neighbours, friends and relatives gathered at the local church followed with a grave side burial at the local cemetery. It was one of the worst days in Gwenny's life. When Gwenny was sitting in the back of the car for the journey home to Southampton, she took her journal out of her bag.

<u>Friday, March 26th</u>

CLEMMIE IS DEAD!!! DEAD! DEAD! He didn't even say goodbye. I can't believe it. Mum said he wouldn't die and he has died. I hate Mum right now and I hate Clemmie for leaving me. How am I going to live without him?

cHAPTER tWENTY-nINE - eXAMINATION

sOUTHAMPTON - bEFORE tREATMENT (1976)

This has been the worst day of my entire life. I've hated every moment. I feel as if I am in recovery after a terrible ordeal. I feel as if I have been assaulted both physically and emotionally. I'm mentally exhausted and every bone in my body is aching with all the squishing, squashing, prodding and poking that I've had to endure. I don't want anyone, not one person to ever touch me again. I feel as if my body has been invaded by strange prying hands. My privacy has been ripped apart. My bloods have been taken so many times. The anger I have had to cover up because not one of those phlebotomists could find a suitable vein. Then, when they did find a vein, they promised me it wouldn't hurt. Wrong! It hurt like hell. I knew it would. I'm fed up of all their soft talk and reassurance. It's all lies!

After that there were the questions, the questions, the questions! I swear the questions went on for hours. They went like this...

Have you any tenderness?

Do you have any persistent pain?

Have you noticed any changes in your breathing?

How many nosebleeds do you have in a day?

Do you need to use the toilet more often?

Have you noticed any hearing loss?

Have you experienced any vision problems?

Do you get any dizziness?

It was like an oral examination in school. But to be honest I felt I had no hope of getting the answers correct. And frankly, after all the indignities I have suffered today, I didn't feel like being helpful anymore. I knew the doctors and nurses were just trying to do their job but I just needed to be left alone.

At one point, I got so upset when I heard that a male consultant was going to physically examine me. That's when I completely freaked out. I was so angry that no one had asked my permission. They seemed to be talking 'at me' not 'to me'. It began to feel like the final insult. Suddenly, the tiny voice inside me blurted out,

'Why can't I have a lady doctor?'

'I'll just go and find out if there is a lady doctor available,' said the nurse.

After she left the room, I was grateful for a few minutes alone with my mum. That's when I burst into tears and sank back into the chair with my hands around my chest trying to protect myself. Mum tried to be sympathetic but it was obvious that she wanted me to change my mind.

'Gwenny…they're all doctors. You're just being silly.'

'But Mum,' I said through gaps in my sobbing, 'I always see a lady doctor at our surgery. I've even waited weeks for an appointment. You know I have.'

Inside my head, I didn't like what I was hearing. My inner voice was saying, 'It's my right. It's my body.' They didn't know how I'd always hated male doctors after that horrendous experience of my finger being stitched, without an anaesthetic, when I was only four years old. I looked at the faded scar on my right hand. That had always been my nightmare. But by the time the nurse returned Mum had somehow persuaded me that I didn't want to wait for another appointment and that I should grit my teeth and bear it.

It reminded me of being a little kid again without any rights. I felt even worse a few minutes later when I was shown into a consulting room and asked to strip off all my clothes apart from my pants, I felt like a prisoner without any choices. Then, when

I tried to pick up my cardigan to cover my chest, I was told to leave it behind the curtains. I felt so exposed, stripped down to my pants walking out from behind the screen. I was so aware of my nakedness. I hunched my shoulders and put my hands in front of my breasts and curled my shoulders with embarrassment. As the male consultant examined me, I tensed up. I even forgot to breathe as he ran his hands all over all my body, front and back, checking for any lumps and bumps. I tried to 'blank off' the whole experience. I tried to think of something that would take my mind off the invasion of my own private body. The examination seemed to go on forever. I loathed every minute.

Mum and I didn't talk on the way home. There was nothing to say.

I was so angry when I got home that I raced up the stairs and locked myself in my bedroom. In temper, I threw all the blankets, and even the mattress, up against the door. Then, I curled myself up tightly and made myself a little nest in the corner, between the bed and the wardrobe. This is where I am sitting now, trying to calm down, trying to cope with it all. I am whispering to myself inside my head that I need time to recover from today. I need to be alone in my own little room, with my own bits and pieces around me. My head is thumping and as I look in my bedroom mirror I can see that my cheeks are very flushed. I know I will have to go back for test results but I will deal with that another day. Today I just need to be peaceful. I can feel my breathing gradually getting back to normal. The smell in my nostrils is still so clinical but if I close my eyes I am becoming aware of the familiar smells of my own room, which has traces of my favourite perfume and my lavender scented sheets. I am home again and I am going to stay here until I feel better.

Dear God,

Please help me cope with my illness. I am trying to remain positive that the

doctors will be able to make me better but it is very hard not to think about dying. God… I don't want to die! I have so much to live for. I haven't managed to print my book of poems. You just can't let me die… not yet!

Also, I haven't seen the world yet and I haven't even got a boyfriend. I haven't had a chance to fall in love. I haven't even done half the things on my 'To do list'… so please don't let me die.

Amen.

P.S. I promise that I will go to church every Sunday when I am better if you just let me live. Amen again.

cHAPTER tHIRTY – lAsT lEtTER

sOUTHAMPTON (1976)

Mum gave me Clemmie's letter which he had placed in the hands of the solicitor. He had written it so that it could be read in the event of his death. He had left it with instructions that I read it before his funeral; I've kept his letter tucked inside my journal. It makes me feel as if he's still talking to me. I've read it a hundred times since his death.

My Dearest Gwenny,

If you are reading this it means that I will have passed away but don't be sad Gwenny. I know that I'll be reunited with my beautiful Annie again. I will be content.

Gwenny, I know you so well… you are such a sensitive little girl but once you have got over the initial shock of my passing, I want you to get on with your life. You are so creative and I want you to use your creativity well.

Firstly, you need to promise me that you will work hard at school especially at your English Literature lessons. Then, remember to write whenever you can. You have a natural talent Gwenny, but your creativity needs to be developed. You have a vivid imagination…use it well. Accept all the help you are offered from your teachers and they will support you in improving your writing. Take their advice and read the works of your favourite poets. Don't forget to study the works of Dylan Thomas, Keats, Byron and any of the other great poets. You will learn something different from them all.

More that anything else… remember how much I love you. You have made me so happy Gwenny; when my Annie died during childbirth, I was devastated to be

a widower at such a young age. Then, a few months later your mother went into labour, and you arrived so quickly that we had no time to even call the midwife. So I had no choice other than to help bring you into this world. Since that moment Gwenny you've been like my own child. We've developed such a special bond.

I have written you into my will; you will inherit all Annie's jewellery when you come of age. Your parents will sell my cottage and they will hopefully use the proceeds to help with your university education. Your mum will be able to continue her teaching career and your dad will be able to expand his printing business. You're lucky to have such caring parents, stay close to them. I know that you and Beth don't always see eye to eye right now; but deep down she really loves you and I know you will be friends eventually.

My dear Gwenny, you are such a talented writer. Just make sure that Dad prints your poems. It will be a book that will give readers such pleasure. People will connect with your work because you write from the heart. I have observed your fascination for the printed word from an early age. It has been amazing to watch. You have so obviously inherited my love of words. Please get your work published while you are still young and don't leave it too late like I did. I could have gone far with my singing. My mum always said I had the voice of an angel but I didn't believe her. I should have gone to London College of Music when I had the chance of a scholarship, but when my father died I couldn't leave my mother.

So Gwenny be a success for me, for yourself and for your family. Don't accept failure, but if you do fail, learn from your mistakes and don't ever be afraid to have another go. Be kind to your mum and dad; they both love you. Mum finds it hard to juggle looking after you all. Always tell her you love her, she needs you to let her know how you feel. Your dad loves you too but he is so blinkered about

making money and making things better for his children that he has forgotten to show you how much he loves you.

My last request is that you read a poem at my funeral. Do this for me. I love the one you wrote for me when you were about eleven years old. I like to think that I will be still watching over you from heaven. You have been and will always be one of the most important people in my life.

Clemmie xxx

'Why do your parents need to move?' Gwenny asked James a few days later.

'My dad's got promotion and it's a good time for us as a family because I can start my 'A' levels at a new college in September,' answered James.

'But it's the other side of the country.'

'I know. But you should understand because your family moved from Wales for your father's printing business so you know what it feels like.'

'Yeah, but we can drive home to Wales in a couple of hours.'

'Well, it's only Newcastle. It's not like we're going to the other side of the world.'

'Yeah but we'll never ever get to see each other.'

'I promise I'll keep in touch… and there's always the school holidays.'

'We'll both be busy studying for our 'A' levels.'

'Listen, I'd rather stay here but my family circumstances mean I have to go…I promised my parents I'd do my best to catch up with my studying. They have worked hard to find us a new home, and a new school where I can study my art 'A' level.'

She nodded and looked down at her hands, picking the tiny bits of skin on her fingers.

'We'll have to write until we can see each other again,'

'This is the worst day of my life.'

'Gwenny Evans... you do exaggerate.'

'What about me?' moaned Gwenny. 'We could have started a new sixth form college together.'

'I thought you were going to a sixth form in a different school. I bet you will pass your English 'A' level with flying colours'.

'I hate English. I hate 'A' levels. I hate everything right now and I especially hate goodbyes. It doesn't have to be like this. My parents would let you live in our spare room.'

'You haven't even got a spare room.'

'We could make you one. You could use Beth's room while she is at university'.

'Well, I might need to do that in the school holidays.'

'Yeah.... pigs might fly.'

'Oh, Gwenny Evans, if only you could hear yourself. You're being completely and utterly unreasonable.'

James rose to leave. He crossed the room, as if to exit and then suddenly stopped, as if he had just remembered something. He opened his duffle bag and carefully took a small cardboard box.

'What's this?' squealed Gwenny, forgetting her anguish for a minute.

But when she opened the outer box she was puzzled by the inner box, it was white with a silver emblem engraved in the centre. She immediately thought it was a bible, or even a prayer book.

'You think it's a bible, don't you?' commented James, grinning.

'No,' she lied.

Then, she opened it and inside was a tiny silver star hung on a fine looped chain, laid on a white satin cushion.

'Oh James, it's gorgeous. But now I feel awful as I don't have anything for you. I only have this… it's my lucky silver three pence,' she said as she removed it from her pocket. 'It's all I've got.'

'No, I couldn't take it, it's yours,' he started but she ignored his pleas. She took his hand and placed the silver three pence in his open palm.

'I want you to have it.'

'Thanks Gwenny Evans I'll always carry it with me,' he promised and inserted it into his wallet. Then, he carefully removed her old necklace from her neck and replaced it with the new one. Gwenny turned away from him, her eyes brimming with tears.

'I'm never going to take it off ever, ever, ever….' she sobbed.

'I'm sorry Gwenny Evans,' whispered James, kissing her lightly on her cheek as he hugged her. Seconds later, he untangled her arms and walked out of the door. Gwenny couldn't believe James was leaving her. She wanted to run after him and plead with him to stay but he had no choice. His family were moving and so she would have to get on with her life. Reluctantly she left the lounge and went upstairs to her bedroom. Her family would be home soon and in her present state she did not feel like talking to anyone.

Once in her room, she inserted the key in the lock and opened her journal. It opened on Clemmie's last letter. Instantly, Clemmie's voice came into in her head. *Write down your feelings.*

She wrote one line.

My heart has just broken into millions of tiny pieces...I am really scared of the future without Clemmie and now without James!

Then, she threw the pen across the room and flung herself onto the bed, buried her face in the pillow and cried. She didn't know who exactly she was crying for...Gwenny just knew that she needed to cry.

cHAPTER tHIRTY-oNE – bLOOD rESULTS

sOUTHAMPTON (1976)

Gwenny had not slept in the car on the way home. She didn't know why but she just felt like crying. She'd had such a lovely time back with her friends in Wales. But it was such a relief when at last Dad drove into their drive. Rosie was the first to get out of the car; she had been sleeping and went straight upstairs. Dad carried Gareth, who was fast asleep, upstairs to bed while Gwenny went into the kitchen where Mum was already sorting through a pile of letters.

'There's one from the hospital,' observed Mum, 'it must be the result of your blood tests Gwenny.'

'Can I open it, Mum?'

'No love, better wait for Dad to come. He won't be a minute.'

'Look at this,' said Dad, a few minutes later, handing the letter to Mum. 'They want Gwenny to go back to the hospital for more tests and an MRI scan.'

'What's an MRI scan?' asked Gwenny, 'I don't like the sound that.'

'It says *magnetic resonance imaging* but I'm not sure what that means. We'll ask them in the morning. Now don't start worrying; it's probably just a routine examination. They have to do these things,' Mum reassured.

'If it's tomorrow morning I won't be able to go. I have to hand in my course work for my mock GCE exam,' insisted Gwenny.

'Don't worry, I'll phone the school to explain,' said Mum. 'I know you've got to be in school, but this letter states that the tests must be repeated as soon as possible. We'll drop your course work off on the way to the hospital.'

Gwenny suddenly felt exhausted. She was so tired that she couldn't be bothered to unpack. She opened up her dressing table drawer and took out one of her oldest nighties. She dragged it over her head and lay down on the bed. But as soon as she put the light out the thoughts in her head, which had been on a back burner all day, suddenly came alive. There was nothing else but to write it all down so she got out her journal and started to scribble.

Sunday

I think I have cancer. Why would they call me back so soon if there wasn't something seriously wrong? I know that my cousin, Tudor had to go back to the hospital for a scan and he had cancer. I know cancer takes forever to treat. I know that the treatment is really harsh. Tudor's treatment went on for years. Oh God… this will mean big changes in my life. I won't be able to go on holiday next year because I'll be ill. I won't be able to go skiing on the school trip. I won't be able to travel back to Wales in the holidays to see my family and friends. I won't be able to do these things because of cancer. I just remembered that Mum said Tudor lost all his hair. Oh my God, I'm going to be bald. How am I going to walk down the street? I'll just be stuck indoors and the bullies will have something else to get me for. I can't attend school with no hair and this will affect my 'O' levels and I won't have any qualifications. I won't be able to go on to the sixth form. And that means that I can't try my 'A' level exams either. My whole life will be ruined because of cancer!

She paused. Her arm was aching from the frantic writing. She rubbed her wrist and began to scribble again.

I might not even get better. I might die. Tudor died. Oh God. Why me? This is driving me crazy… that's all I can think about; a future with cancer. I am angry with the changes it will bring to my life. I don't know if I am imagining it? But am I normally so white and pale? I keep hearing Mum's voice in my head saying 'Gwenny, you look so tired.' I know I always feel tired, that's why I had the blood tests before we went to Wales. I know I am constantly exhausted. I feel like I want to run away but if I have cancer it will come with me. There is no escape this time. My cousin had cancer. My grandmother had cancer. What are the chances of me escaping cancer? Oh God...what have I done to deserve this?

Gwenny lay back on her pillow. She was still shocked at her thoughts but gradually her panic was subsiding as more rational ones took over. She began writing again.

I may not have cancer, it could be something else. They could have made a mistake. Maybe, I won't need anymore tests. But strangely enough these words don't bring me any comfort. My inner voice is shouting louder inside my head. What about the aches in my legs and hips? What about the constant ulcers in my mouth? What about the never ending nosebleeds? What about the bruises? What about the constant tiredness?

Gwenny decided that sleep was impossible, with her head in such a whirl, so she put the light on and looked up the words she didn't understand in her dictionary. What was oncology, phlebotomy, radiotherapy, chemotherapy? These were all words she had heard before when Tudor was ill but she didn't really understand what they meant. She couldn't go back to sleep after reading about these words but she knew that she couldn't cope with doing nothing. She picked up her pen and started writing.

This is my list of questions that I would like to ask the hospital doctor.

> *'What's wrong with me?'*
>
> *'How long will I have to stay in hospital?'*
>
> *'Will I be able to go to school?'*
>
> *'Will my hair fall out straightaway?'*
>
> *'Can I travel to Wales?'*

Then she paused, bit her bottom lip and closed the diary, locked it with a key, replaced her key on the chain around her neck and turned out the light. There was still one burning question racing through in her mind.

'Am I going to die?

The next day she met her consultant for the first time.

'Hello Gwenny, do come in. My name is Doctor Neville. I think I saw you briefly once before. I'm one of the paediatric consultants. Please take a seat.'

She walked nervously across the room. She stole glances trying to catch his eyes. His expression remained blank. His face gave nothing away, although he seemed to be avoiding her eyes. Then, slowly and deliberately he sat down on the chair behind the desk. She sat opposite him and looked directly at him. He rustled his papers and then, as if changing his mind, he got up from behind his desk and pulled up a chair by her side. He lent forward facing her, he was clenching his hands. She could tell he was very nervous.

' Gwenny,' he started, 'I know you have been waiting for these results and I apologise that it has taken so long… but I had the lab re-run the tests because I wanted to make sure that we had your correct diagnosis.'

'But you asked to see me alone without my parents?' questioned Gwenny.

'Yes. I treat all my teenage patients like this. Your parents have agreed to me speaking to you first. I'll talk to them as soon as I have spoken to you.'

He paused again.

'Gwenny, I know that you asked me to be truthful and I want to be completely honest with you. So today I want you to prepare yourself for some very bad news. There is no easy way for me to say this to you. You have cancer!'

ePILOGUE

(cHILDREN'S cANCER wARD) aUGUST (1979)

I was a little bit scared today. I was back at the hospital for my appointment at day clinic. As I walked down the corridor I was aware of a young girl sitting in one of the single wards. She had no hair, no eyebrows and her pallor was deathly white. Dr Neville came up to me. He had just arrived on the ward for the day clinic.

'Hi Gwenny,' he greeted.

I smiled. I'm always pleased to see Dr Neville. He had completely changed the way I feel about male doctors.

'Yes, I've heard your good news. Third year in remission… you've done so well Gwenny. So you're all ready to go to university?'

'Yes, just two weeks to go. I'm going on holiday with my friends first and then I'm leaving home! Yeah!'

I could see that he noticed me glancing at the young girl in my old room.

'You've seen our newest little patient then. Her name is Ruth. She's fifteen years old. In fact, she's the same age as you were when you first came to this ward. She also has the same type of leukaemia that you had.'

'Poor kid.'

'I know you're waiting for your blood tests today so if you have the time, do you think you could have a little word with Ruth? She is pretty down right now and as usual there are not many teenagers to talk to.'

'What will I say?' 'Anything…tell her how you coped with the treatment. Tell her how frustrated the doctors made you feel… relate some of your funny stories… explain to her about your writing, how you've continued your studies and your plans to go to university… but more than anything else… tell her what it's like to feel well again. Reassure her that she too will get better.'

'Okay, I'll do it now… if you think it would help.'

Dr Neville opened the exterior door and tapped lightly on the inner door.

'Hi Ruthie, how's my favourite patient? I have a visitor for you, if you don't mind. This is Gwenny, the young lady, I was telling you about. She's the one who gave us all the trouble when she was fifteen years old.'

'Don't believe his stories. I was a model patient,' I called out to Ruth.

'I have a clinic now… so is it alright… if she comes to talk to you for a few minutes?'

Ruth nodded and I walked into my old single room again. It was the same room that had been my isolation unit but somehow it felt a lot smaller. I couldn't help noticing how things in the room hadn't changed. The identical hospital bed with the oxygen cylinder lined up next to the head of the bed. The thermometer and blood pressure gauge holders attached to the wall. It even had the same smell. I inhaled deeply. I could never forget the clinical aroma. Remembering so many things; I automatically looked up … even the same crack in the ceiling, where the tiles didn't quite meet. I had spent a long time lying in this bed, I knew how many lights there were, how many squares of ceiling tiles. I even knew why there was a little stain on one tile. It was when I'd thrown my drink at the wall and some had splashed on the ceiling. The faded red *Ribena* stain was still visible.

I sat on the edge of the bed and waited for Ruth to speak; she wanted to know everything. It was like she hadn't spoken to anyone else in days. We talked and talked and I was able to answer all her worries and concerns.

'You will get better too,' I reassured Ruth, finally, giving her a hug. 'Shall I come and see you again before I start my university course?'

'Yes please. I'd love to chat with you again. You've helped me so much,' answered Ruth, smiling for the first time in weeks.

sHEFFIELD uNIVERSITY, sEPTEMBER (1979)

I didn't imagine arriving at university like this. I'm scared that no one will speak to me. I'm panicking that I will not be able to cope with the work. I'm frightened that I will not make any friends. I'm scared about everything and I want to go home. I really want to… but I know I won't. I won't give up! I never do!

My room is lovely. It's on the ground floor which is brilliant. The furniture is brand new and I've even got my own shower room. I'm happy and sad all at the same time. It was hard saying goodbye to my family but I was determined not to stay in my room alone so I knocked on the doors next to mine and met my new neighbours. We agreed to meet for our first evening meal together at the entrance to the canteen.

Meanwhile, I wheeled myself down to the university library to get some books from the reading list before anyone else did. There were so many books I felt like I was on cloud nine. Then, I saw him out of the corner of my eye. He was carrying a pile of books. I swear my heart missed a beat. It can't be… but it is, a little older and more mature: James Harrington! Here at the same university as me!
Oh my God! He's here. I can scarcely breathe. I can hardly hold the books on my lap because my knees are shaking. I suddenly realise that my feelings for James haven't changed one little bit. In fact, I now believe the saying *Absence makes the heart grow fonder.* I just know he is the one I want to spend the rest of my life with! I suddenly felt I needed to hold the star I am wearing around my neck. I pull it out from under my blouse and placed it in front of my jumper. I have never taken it off since the last

time I saw him three years ago.

'Hey, I'm sorry,' he started to apologise, as he and his pile of books, almost tripped over me and my wheel chair.

'I didn't mean to walk into you but I didn't see you down there.'

I looked up at his face, smiling. He stared back, he had puzzled expression, as if he couldn't quite believe his eyes.

'Hi James,' I murmured, looking up from under my fringe. I could feel my eyes filling up with tears.

'Hello…do I know you?' he hesitated and then with a sudden realisation, 'It's you isn't it? I thought I recognised the lovely accent.'

His face lit up. Our eyes locked into a long and loving stare. Neither of us uttered a word, too afraid to spoil the moment. Then, he placed his pile of books on the floor so he could see me properly and said,

'Hello Gwenny Evans… it's so good to see you again.'

I felt he meant it. My heart was now racing. I felt sick with the strength of my emotions.

'I just can t believe it…. it's you… you're really here… you're at the same university as me… Wow!' he stuttered, shaking his head in disbelief 'I honestly never thought I would see you again…ever.'

'I tried to contact you James,' I whispered…. 'but you didn't answer…you didn't reply.'

'Hey, that's not true…you didn't write to me Gwenny Evans! I didn't even receive one letter from you and I wrote to you almost every day at first. I didn't have much money so my mum always offered to post the letters to you. She often commented what a shame it was that you didn't reply.'

'But…but James. I wrote letters and letters but they were always marked '*Return to sender'*. So I thought you must have moved house, so started printing '*Please forward to new address'* but even then they were returned '*Not known at this address'* signed by someone called '*M. Blair'*.

'What's that? Say that again. My mum's maiden name was Blair… Margaret Blair.'

There was a moment of silence and then James continued,

'Oh no... I'm so sorry that signature proves it was my mother. I can't believe she would do it. She knew how devastated I was that you didn't write. She witnessed my unhappiness and all the time she was keeping us apart.'

He paused, as if reflecting.

'I thought of you every day. I wanted to come and see you… only Mum warned me not to make a fool of myself over a girl, who obviously didn't want to keep in touch. She even hinted that you might have got another boyfriend.'

He glanced away, as if he was wiping a stray eyelash with his fingers and then he turned to face me.

'Well, she can't keep us apart any longer. I am finally independent of my over protective parents. It was my eighteenth birthday a few weeks ago and I inherited my grandfather's fortune so I have just bought myself a house in Sheffield near the university.'

I was unable to answer as my mind worked overtime. He was independent. He was no longer answerable to his parents. I smiled.

'But enough of me,' continued James. 'What are you studying? No… don't tell me. Let me guess…English Literature, isn't it?

I nodded.

'And you?'

'History of Art.'

'Yes, Art ... of course.'

'Wow, Gwenny Evans. This is going to be the best university course ... ever. But hey, how are you? Are you better? How come you're in a wheel chair?'

'Thought I'd give my legs a rest today but apart from that I'm fine. I don't have cancer anymore but what about you? You look so well. Are you in remission too?'

He smiled and nodded. He got down to my level. I sensed that he still cared about me. He had that wicked glint in his eye again. He removed the books from my lap and stretched his big strong arms around my skinny frame.

'Gwenny Evans? Please may I kiss you?'

'Oh James… you don't have to ask.'

'Thank you my little *'Miskin'* girl. I'm going to enjoy getting to know you even better this time.'

He kissed me on my cheek, he hugged me with so much passion.

'Ouch!' I unexpectedly murmured.

'Oh God ... did I hurt you? I'm so sorry.'

'No, its ok, you just brushed against my leg. My right leg's in plaster.'

I removed the rug to show him.

'Don't laugh. I fell down some stairs while on holiday and broke my leg. Don't you dare ask if I was drunk! The wheel chair is only temporary until I get used to the crutches.'

'Whoa… you had me there. I thought I was going to have to spend the next three years looking after you by pushing you around in a wheelchair.'

‘Well, I won’t be in a wheelchair; but I could certainly do with someone to look after me,’ I flirted encouragingly.

At that moment, it seemed like the world stood still. There was no sound from anywhere. He looked at me, his eyes fixed on the silver star necklace around my neck. I blocked out my surroundings. There was me. There was James. Suddenly, nothing else on earth mattered. The attraction between us was undeniable. The atmosphere was electric. I gazed at him, not losing eye contact for a moment. Inside my head my inner voice dared him to say the words I’d been longing to hear *‘Go on. Go on. Ask me. Ask me. I will say yes. I will say yes.’*

I held my silver star and wished harder that I have ever wished before. My heart flipped and flopped ten times over. He looked at me longingly. He stared at my eyes hoping they would indicate what to say next. It was as if he was trying to read my mind. Then, the world actually did stand still. He took out the silver three pence, that I had given him all those years ago, from the inside pocket of his coat. He pressed it into my open palm and said…

‘Gwenny Evans, will you do me the honour of becoming my wife?’

I have already written the lines. The words are already in my head and like every good love story. I know that we will live happily ever after… not yet planning our wedding, not yet planning how many babies we will have… those things will come later … we will be planning the words and illustrations for our next book of poems… love poems!

‘Our hands touched, our hearts met, love happened…’

Poems that Gwenny wrote throughout her life…

My dad has a printing press

The printing shed greets me with sounds of

Clunking and clanging.

The air is filled with smells of...

Grease and oil,

Paraffin and wax

The treadle creaks and turns,

As rollers meet plates.

And ink meets paper.

Regal and proud the printing press dominates its space,

Overshadowing me with its size and sound,

Making me feel so small and insignificant,

Yet fascinated and delighted...

My dad has a printing press

No more

No more holding my hand,

Or singing with the band.

No more going on walks,

Or having our special talks.

No more having fun,

Or days out in the sun.

Now my eyes are all red,

Cos my Clemmie is dead!

Silence

Silence… I love it!

I have longed for the silence of home and the comfort of my own small bedroom,

Where there are no wires that connect me to the drugs that keep me alive.

No beeps from the bags of saline,

No flickering lights that glow in the dark,

No sounds of children whimpering in their sleep,

No coughing, no snoring,

No distant voices as the nurses go about their nightly duties,

No doctors appearing for emergency patients,

No night porters wheeling trolleys,

No scratchy bed sheets,

No footsteps on uncarpeted floors,

Only peace and tranquillity,

This is exactly what I need right now.

I am home.

The Sea

I went to Mumbles and swam in the sea,

Me and Clemmie, Clemmie and me.

We laughed and laughed as we ran on the sand,

Me with Clemmie, holding his hand

Then the tide came in and my clothes got wet,

The day by the sea, I'll never forget!

Frozen in time

I am frozen in time...

Silent like the whisper in the early morning dawn,

I am shocked by the news that I have just received.

It has not sunk in at all.

It is far too complicated.

I just wanted to live in peace,

But suddenly in just one tiny second

My world has been turned upside down, back to front and inside out.

It is a shambles, a mess and I know that inside I am falling to pieces.

Suddenly, there is no firm foundation for my feet to stand on.

No security of my home to run to...

Just the future rambling on, with my whole life out of control...

I have cancer.

Blood transfusions

I have never seen a bag of blood before,

It looks much darker red and comes in a flat bag.

It takes ages to drip it into my body but once it starts taking effect

I actually begin to feel like I have more energy again!

But ...*I will never get over the fact*

That...*someone has given their blood for* **me** *to stay alive.*

*I will never be able to thank them enough...b****ecause now I will not die!***

Snow

Stranded and wild...the snow swirls around my face,

Each feathery snowflake so tiny and yet so perfect,

Creating a mass of whirling whiteness

Branches bend and groan with the unexpected weight,

As a velvety blanket of white alters the landscape,

I stand by the open window...mesmerized, unable to drag myself away,

Snowflakes stick to my tongue

And I taste their icy chill as they slowly dissolve in my mouth.

Nosebleed

Drips of red cover my page,

Alarm in my heart... will it stop?

A heavier flow with bright red tissues.

Panic rises now... will it stop?

Clothes and bed covers stained with colour,

Fear creeps in now... will it stop?

Ice packs bowls and newly gloved hands,

Worry now... will it stop?

At last... it lessens... no more bleeding,

Sighs of relief now,

The nosebleed stops.

The poems Gwenny wrote about falling in love with James…

Poem for James

Your eyes are like deep pools of the bluest water,

You have the most beautiful eyes that I have ever seen.

When I met you for the very first time

I began to feel alive.

And…as I stood next to you…I was…

Mesmerized by the intensity of your stare.

You opened my eyes to unknown feelings,

New pathways, fresh horizons, endless possibilities,

And… at that moment I tumbled head over heels in love with you!

In love with James

Sunbeams shoot from my heart.

Can you feel the warmth?

Firecrackers explode in my head.

Can you hear their sound?

Electric shocks as I touch your skin.

Can you experience the shockwaves?

My whole body has come alive.

I am so in love with you James.

Falling in love

Never have I experienced such a deep and intense feeling,

It was all about you.

I was transformed by your beauty, your handsomeness;

You spoke my name like no other,

Your eyes did not leave mine.

I was helplessly full of emotions that I had never come across before,

I didn't know it then but it was inevitable,

I was falling head of heels in love with you.

Missing you already

As you walk away, I am missing you already.

When did you become such an important part of my life?

We met, we chatted and suddenly I found a friend in you,

Someone who is completely tuned into the way I feel,

Someone who is going through the same things at the same time as me,

Someone who manages to keep their sense of humour,

Someone who in spite of everything else hangs on to the gift of life;

James… you have become one of the most important people in my whole world.

And then there was you…

You walked into my life and you stayed,

You cared,

You supported,

You listened,

You were always there for me.

There was never anyone else like you before,

You walked into my life and you stayed

Our hands touched…

Our hearts met…

Love happened.

Thank you to the following businesses for their help with the printing this book…

Stanbury /Chameleon Printers, Gosport

Sarah Rees - Cover to Cover, Mumbles

Morgans, Swansea

A. and J. Lawrence

Swansea Grand Theatre

Glamorgan Cricket and Cricket Wales

T for Two

South-West Trains

Wightlink

Finally, thank you to all my family and friends, who have attended my fundraising events and donated many raffle prizes so that I could raise the money to print this book.

Return to Miskin by Alyson Young

The sequel to *Miskin Girl*

Follow the story of Gwenny as she becomes engaged to James. Will their romance survive university life? What career path will Gwenny follow… poet or journalist? How many more poems does Gwenny write? Can Gwenny achieve her dream of writing a book of love poems?

James and Gwenny are both in remission after undergoing cancer treatment but do they relapse? Will they eventually marry? Does James become the artist he always wanted to be? Read the continuing saga in ***Return to Miskin.***